HE WASN'T READY FOR THE ULTIMATE TOUCHDOWN IN THE SKY

It was a beautiful day. His knee was better. Joe was almost ready for the big game.

As he cycled home from the Malibu hills, a modest camper left the beach followed by an old Ford van filled with tanned, teenage surfers. Joy-riding, buzzed on wine, the van played at passing. They were still jockeying for first as they entered the tunnel.

Pedaling easily, Joe entered from the opposite end. Suddenly there was the screech of rubber, the scrape of metal, the shattering of glass. When the van skidded out, Joe's bike lay mangled, riderless on the battered hood. Was it all over, or had it just begun?

JOE'S STILL GOT A LOT TO DO AND . . .

HEAVEN CAN WAIT

HEAVEN CAN WAIT

WARREN BEATTY	JULIE CHRISTIE	JAMES MASON

CHARLES GRODIN	DYAN CANNON	BUCK HENRY

VINCENT GARDENIA   &   JACK WARDEN

Screenplay by ELAINE MAY, WARREN BEATTY and BUCK HENRY

Produced by WARREN BEATTY

Directed by WARREN BEATTY AND BUCK HENRY

A PARAMOUNT PICTURE

HEAVEN CAN WAIT

A novel by

Leonore Fleischer

Based on a screenplay by
Elaine May, Warren Beatty
and Buck Henry

BALLANTINE BOOKS · NEW YORK

ISBN 0-345-27665-5

Manufactured in the United States of America

First Edition: June 1978

For Tom Durbin and auld lang syne.

CHAPTER I

    This was the time of the day that Joe loved best, the hours before the morning had been burnished to a gleam. When he rolled out of bed at first light, there was still a chill in the canyon air, and the moon was only just disappearing reluctantly from the pink sky. The day smelled fresh and newborn and ready for anything; Joe could sense it. He grinned as he moved around his small house, performing the routine that always started his day.

First he opened his tiny refrigerator and took out the makings of his breakfast. He wouldn't be eating for hours; Joe Pendleton never ate a mouthful before his morning exercises. Who could run or jump on a full stomach? And Joe believed that the digestive system went into shock when hot or cold food was tossed into it, so he placed the eggs and the oranges in a small bowl and poured a Pyrex cup full of skim milk. By the time he came back to the house, they'd be at room temperature for his grateful intestinal tract.

Next he switched on his little Sony radio and listened to the weather report as he pulled on his gray sweatpants and hooded sweatshirt and laced up his running shoes. The temperature in Los Angeles would be seventy degrees later on and dry; now it was fifty-two. After listening to the weather report, he flipped the dial over to KHJ and turned the volume down. Rock and roll was the right tempo for his warm-up, but first thing in the morning it was a little heavy on his ears.

Bending and stretching, Joe worked the sleep kinks out of his muscles, moving with the grace of a dancer. After fifteen minutes of stretches, he picked up a white nylon rope with weighted handles and a digital counter in one end. The rope was extra-long to accommodate his six feet four inches. After skipping rope for ten minutes, he he threw the rope on the bed and jogged in place for five minutes. By now he could feel his pulse rate begin to rise and the nervous, oxygenated energy course through him. He jogged toward the front door, pushed it open, and ran free into the morning.

It was so clear you could see the ocean glinting down at Malibu. Joe ran easily along the fire-trail that snaked through Topanga Canyon, through the drought-dry brush and the dusty eucalyptus. His long legs eating up the ground at a steady rate, he was attuned to every part of his body. Especially the right knee. As he ran, he actually *became* the knee; its every movement, every sensation, a part of all of him. It was okay. It was really okay.

It hadn't always been okay. For six months he'd been benched because of that damn knee, sitting out the games and watching Jarrett on the field playing Joe's position. The knee had been bad, bad enough to keep him out of the games and, for a while, bad enough to keep him on his back. There had been talk of surgery, but one thing Joe Pendleton knew was that surgeons *always* talked of surgery. And the orthopedic surgeons on call to the Los Angeles Rams might have been the best in the world, but they were still sawbones looking for a bone to saw. Look at Namath.

Joe thought about Namath and said no to surgery. Loud and clear and often, until the doctors with their painkillers and their injections had finally backed off and washed their hands of him. They still checked him out every week, though, and every week Joe had made some small progress, using his own methods of tightening those loose ligaments. Exercise, exercise, and more exercise.

2

Meanwhile, the Rams were hot, even with Joe Pendleton out as quarterback. The season had gotten off to a strong start, and by their first appearance on Monday Night Football it looked as though the Rams might be going all the way. The defense was tough and fast and the offense had been sparked by Tom Jarrett, a twenty-seven-year old Minnesotan with a long arm and a fast eye. By the time the Rams left for their last road game of the season, everybody was saying they'd be clinching the Western Division of the National Football Conference. They were averaging twenty-one points a game and they had the best win-loss record in the Conference, ten and two. It looked like Super Bowl year, it really did.

And Joe had been out of it. Working on his knee, he'd missed almost the entire regular season, although in the past two weeks he'd been working out with the team in practice. His knee felt good now, really good, and his arm was as strong as ever. As he ran down the canyon trail, feeling the dry earth packed hard under his feet and seeing the erosion eating away the banks of the outcroppings, he thought about football. For a change, he grinned to himself.

At thirty-four, Joe Pendleton was one of the top quarterbacks in pro football.

He had a sixth sense for the game. Jarrett was good. He was young and fast and had good lateral movement. He'd done a damn fine job of substituting. But, he was inexperienced; he didn't have the seasoning that only many years in the pros could bring. And that meant that the coach had to send the plays in from the bench.

When Joe was in there, it was *his* game. He read the defensive formations; he pinpointed the weaknesses and he called the plays. Pendleton could have been one of the all-time greats, like Unitas or Tarkenton . . . still could be . . . if he could lead the Rams all the way to the Super Bowl. He had just never had a shot at it.

Ironic, he thought, as he turned at the foot of the canyon and began to run back up the fire-trail. Now that his team was having a damn near perfect season, it was Jarrett who was sparking them. Jarrett, seven years younger. Jarrett, who had all those good years left, while Joe . . . he shook his head to get rid of the thought. In the first place, it was unworthy of a team player. In the second place, Joe would get his chance, he was sure of it. His knee was good, he was looking good in the practice sessions. He felt good.

He ran silently, enjoying the warmth of the sun on his shoulders, the feeling that his heart was pumping away strongly, and all his limbs were functioning well. Joe was proud of his body, especially when it was in top shape. It did his bidding; the arm worked perfectly, getting that pigskin into the hands of the receiver; the legs worked perfectly, running, faking. The eye was true. Joe was proud, and he worked hard at keeping in shape.

Living alone as he did in a small house—more of a cabin, really—near the top of Topanga Canyon, Joe had lots of time to think, especially in the last few months when he wasn't playing football. He thought about what he wanted out of life. What should a guy like him want? What *did* a guy like him want? It came down to the same thing every time—the chance to win for the Rams in the Super Bowl. Love? Marriage? Kids? Somehow they weren't in the picture. Someday, sure, but not now, and not with any of the ladies he knew or had known.

There were ladies, naturally, not too many, but pretty ones. Once a lady had even moved into Topanga for a little while; just friends; it was her idea, not Joe's. He knew in advance how it would end. Somehow they never understood what made a guy like Joe tick. They all thought that football was glamorous, exciting. But a man's whole life? Sooner or later Joe's long training sessions made them mad. They hated going home at ten o'clock when they wanted to be out boogeying at On-The-Rocks. They never expected to be spending their evenings watching NFL highlights in sixteen millimeter and, most of all, they hated Joe's blender and every nourishing wet concoction he produced in it. Blenders ought to be used for piña coladas and frozen daiquiries, not alfalfa sprout shakes. There were some things about Joe Pendleton it was hard to say goodbye to . . . the unruly black hair, the bright blue eyes, the wide, white heartbreaking smile, the muscles . . . but the blender! Yechhhh!

It was good to have the house to himself, actually. He was territorial. Once a girl had insisted that the last half of the only avocado in the house should go into her facial mask instead of into his blender. He hated arguments. He saved all his negative energy for the opposing team.

Joe's thoughts returned to Tom Jarrett. He hadn't thrown an interception in four games, and the defense had backed him up. Now they were back from Philadelphia, having won against the Eagles; one more victory for the Rams combined with a loss for the 49ers and they would clinch a playoff spot. Their competition would certainly be Dallas. And if they could beat Dallas . . . the Super Bowl! The thought made him shiver. The Super Bowl.

Reaching the house he slowed his pace and ran around it three times, slower each time, to wind down from the long run. Then, bushed and ravenous, he ran inside and turned the shower on full blast. Stripping off his sweatshirt, he dumped it on the bathroom floor, followed by his sweatpants, his sweatsocks and running shoes. Then he ducked under the blast of hot water, cringing at the full force of the steam. It took him a minute before he could actually stand up to the temperature and, once he could take the hot, he turned it off and ran only the cold. Then hot, then cold again. Then out. His body tingled from the shock of the temperature changes and he felt marvelous. Starving, but marvelous.

The eggs and oranges were warm now to the touch. Joe broke the eggs into the blender and cut the oranges into quarters. Into the blender container went a teaspoonful of brewer's yeast, two tablespoons of wheat germ, and three of blackstrap molasses. Then the skim milk. Munching on an orange section, peel and all, Joe threw the blender switch and got out two big glasses. The blender bubbled and whirled and the liquid inside turned a viscous, muddy brown. Yummy. Some people added honey, but not Joe. Honey was sugar and sugar was poison, as bad as coffee, as bad as cigarettes.

He drank his breakfast slowly while thinking over the day ahead. It was a big one for him, a long practice session with the team on the field. He knew they'd be looking him over carefully to see how well his knee was functioning, judging whether or not he'd slowed down any. He realized that Corkle, the trainer, was on his side, and maybe even the coach. But the doctors were dubious, and the owners . . . well, the owners couldn't afford to make mistakes where big money was concerned. Joe knew that Gene Bradley, the owner, would be on the sidelines today, watching the practice sessions. With the season drawing to a close, time was more precious than ever to everybody concerned, and Joe had an anxious moment wondering whether he'd get to play this season at all, this season that might be the Rams' best in years.

A pang took him at the thought that his team might get to the Super Bowl without him. Had he worked so hard to get in shape for nothing? No, never for nothing. It was worth it, every stab of pain that had racked him at first, when he'd worked out for long hours in all kinds of weather. It had been worth it. Look at him now. He was maybe in the best shape he'd been in for years.

He drank the second glassful. It was still early. He

had time to get down to the Coliseum and run a few sprints before practice began.

Bradley stood watching the Rams running plays. It was a light workout today. No body contact was allowed now; the bodies were too valuable to be risked in a practice session. Instead, a light touch of the player's hand was used to show that a block or a tackle had been successful. At his side stood Judson, the head coach, thoughtfully smoking a cigarette, his eyes never leaving the field. The general manager of the Rams, Ed Figarello, stood off to one side, watching carefully, his mind ticking off comments and criticisms, praise and blame, to be portioned out in the locker room after the session. Next to Judson stood Max Corkle, one of the Rams' trainers. *His* eyes were only on Joe Pendleton, who wore a red fishnet "don't-touch-the-quarterback" tank shirt over his football jersey. Joe had just completed a screen pass for a fifteen yard gain.

"Lookin' good, isn't he?" Max remarked to Judson.

"What?" Bradley turned his head at the question, vaguely impatient.

"Pendleton, he's lookin' awful good," Corkle exclaimed.

Bradley shot a quick look at the field. "Yeah," he said without enthusiasm. With Dallas on his mind, he had little thought to spare for a quarterback with a bad right knee.

But Judson had been watching Pendleton, too, and he liked what he was seeing. Now he threw the cigarette down and ground it out carefully with the heel of his cleated shoe. "I think maybe I'll start him Sunday," he said slowly.

Bradley looked startled. "What about Jarrett?" he demanded.

"Pendleton's lookin' better," Judson replied softly.

"He's lookin' awful good," Corkle echoed, beaming.

The owner gave a short, harsh laugh. "Corkle, you

really are something. You wanna be the guy to tell that to Jarrett?"

Now Figarello put in his two cents' worth. "Yeah, Corkle, Pendleton's looking good for having been on the injured list for six months," he said heatedly. He was a big fan of Tom Jarrett's.

"Wait a minute." Judson put up his hand to stop all further argument. "You're the owner, Mr. Bradley," he said significantly.

Bradley nibbled at his lower lip, watching the field with narrowed eyes. Pendleton's arm looked strong, and he was certainly moving that ball.

"What about Pendleton's knee?" he asked finally.

"What about it?" Corkle's chin went up in stubborn loyalty.

"Is he still on cortisone?" Judson demanded.

"Nope." Corkle shook his head.

"Darvon? Xylocaine? *Any* painkillers?" Painkillers slowed a man down and took away his lust for victory.

"Nothing," Corkle said firmly.

"He's lookin' awful good," Judson admitted, with a glance at Bradley.

Silence fell for a minute as each man's thoughts turned to next Sunday, to Dallas, and beyond Dallas to the Super Bowl itself. Any decision made now would have to be the right one. The crunch was on.

Bradley drew a deep breath. "Well, Coach, I'm not gonna interfere with any decision of yours. If you want to start Pendleton against Dallas, start him. But I have to say that I never saw a knee heal like that without surgery before."

On the practice field, Joe feinted back quickly and completed a forty-five yard pass into the end zone.

"He's lookin' awful good," said Judson again.

"That's all I said," Corkle agreed trying to restrain his enthusiasm.

Winded but happy, Joe eased his helmet off and trotted from the practice field. It had been a good session—hard, fast, demanding, but exhilarating. He felt ready. Now for a long shower and a rubdown, then home to relax a few hours.

"Joe, hey, Joe!"

Pendleton turned. Ned Miller, a sportswriter for the L.A. *Times,* was puffing and chugging to catch up with him. Joe slowed his long-legged stride down until Miller came abreast. "Hi. How ya doing?"

"Pretty good," panted the newspaperman. "How's the knee?"

"Terrific," Joe replied easily. He could see the other man looking at him closely, trying to detect the smallest sign of a limp that he could report to his readers.

"Whaddya think of the Rams' chances?" asked Miller.

"I think we're gonna get to the Super Bowl, and I think we're gonna win," Joe answered easily.

"No, but off the record, do you really think you got a chance?"

What did he mean by "you"? Joe wondered. Did he mean you the Rams plural or you Joe Pendleton singular? "Off the record? I think we're going to get to the Super Bowl, and I think we're going to win."

The newspaperman had heard all this before. What he was looking for was a story, not a between-halves pep talk. "Sure, sure. But what do you think of your competition?"

Joe stopped walking. He wasn't born yesterday and he knew precisely what Miller was fishing for. He turned a blank, totally innocent face to the reporter. "My competition?" he asked, as if testing an unfamiliar word.

"Jarrett."

Pushing a wide, boyish smile onto his face, Joe addressed the newspaperman gently, as if instructing a child. "Jarrett's not my competition. My competition is twenty-five other teams. Jarrett is our starting quarterback." Next question.

"Are you saying you think you're ready to start?" persisted Miller. There was a story here somewhere.

"Off the record?" Joe grinned. "I think we're gonna get to the Super Bowl, and I think we're gonna win." He tilted his head at the reporter as if he had just given him the quote of the year, and headed for the locker room, his helmet swinging from his hand.

Miller stared after him, checking one more time for the nonexistent limp. Snotty bastard. Still, he was looking mighty good out there this afternoon. That was some kinda story, at least.

Max Corkle chuckled to himself as he pulled his LTD into Joe's tiny driveway. Boyohoboy, would Joe be surprised! He glanced fondly at the big bakery box on the seat beside him and gave it a pat. Then he cut the engine, stepped out of the car, gave his Rams cap a twitch, unzipped his Rams windbreaker, and picking up the cake box, pushed open the door to Joe's little house. It was never locked. Who'd drive this far up the canyon for absolutely nothing? A bicycle . . . a radio . . . a jump rope and some weights. Joe lived more simply than any pro football player Corkle had ever met.

The house was dark, except for a flickering light in the living room. It would have been silent, too, except for the sound of a saxophone trying to make its uncertain way through "Sweet Georgia Brown." Max put the cake box down on the kitchen counter and peeked around the corner into the living room. Joe was stretched out on the sofa, diddling on his sax, deeply intent on the film he was projecting on the shaky home screen.

It was a black and white film, sixteen millimeter and silent. Max recognized it as one of the game films that teams exchanged among themselves as a courtesy and a convenience. What Joe was glued to was the Dallas defense; he was watching their coverage of the field. Every couple of minutes, he'd stop "Georgia" in the middle of a note and take a long pull at the tall glass of brown liquid he was sipping.

In the kitchen, Max unwrapped the cake, wincing whenever Joe blew a wrong note, which was more often than not. The blender container was half filled with what looked like a chocolate milkshake. Great. Max loved sweets, especially chocolate. He turned on the blender to whip up a head of foam on the milkshake.

Joe turned his head at the noise from the kitchen. "Max?" he called.

"Yeah," Corkle called back. He stopped the blender and brought the container to his lips.

"How ya doin'?" Joe called.

But the shake never made it past the nose. Yecccc-hhhh! Max set it down as if it were rattler venom. "What *is* this brown guck?" he asked in a strangled voice.

"That? It's mainly whipped liver . . ."

"Liver?!" croaked Max, his stomach doing loops.

"Yeah, and whey and alfalfa sprouts, and bean curd, and molasses, and bran and spinach mold . . ."

But Max had stopped listening. It was more than the human gut should be required to bear. A shudder came over him as he remembered how close he'd been to touching the container to his own personal lips. He turned his attention to the cake. Cake! Now *that* was food.

It was a birthday cake, large, round, and smothered in butter cream frosting. The frosting was yellow, and bright blue roses (blue for a boy) splashed across the top of it, curling around the green lettering that spelled out "Happy Birthday, Joe." Corkle examined it reverently. It was gorgeous. Carefully, he placed one candle on it, dead center, between the *h* and the *d* in "birthday." He lit the candle, and picking up the cake, carried it ceremonially into the living room. In a high nasal voice, he began to sing.

"Happy birthday to you,
Happy birthday to you,

Happy birthday, dear Joeeeeee,
Happy birthday toooo yooooo."

Joe slowly rose to his feet, a big smile on his face. "Gee, Max, I didn't think anybody knew! Thanks. Hey, thanks." He lifted his chess set carefully off the coffee table and set it down on the couch so that Corkle would have room for the cake. Then, perching on the sofa, he leaned forward to make a birthday wish on the single candle.

Let me start against Dallas. Please let me start against Dallas. Joe blew out the candle.

"Thanks for coming over, Max," he said gently. He was really touched by Corkle's gesture.

Now it was Corkle's turn to be embarrassed. "Well, I hope you have a lot more, kid," he said gruffly, and headed back into the kitchen for plates and forks.

Joe got up and turned off the projector, then snapped on the overhead lights. The cake stared up at him, large and luscious and loaded with white sugar and artificial color and gums and cholesterol and stabilizers and other yummy additives. He gulped and closed his eyes for a moment, shuddering. Then he contemplated his birthday cake again, as a symbol this time. It meant one year older.

"You want to know something?" he called out to Max in the kitchen. "At my age—in any other business —I'd be a young man."

"Yeah," Corkle called back, "but look at it this way. Pretty soon you can get into another business. You can have a *real* life."

A *real* life? What was Corkle talking about? What was unreal about football? What other life did Joe know? Or understand? Or want, for that matter? "A real life?" he said slowly. "I don't know what that means. This is the only life that's *real* to me. I'm stuck with it."

Corkle came back in from the kitchen, carrying plates, forks and napkins, and a long knife to cut the

12

cake with. "What do you mean, stuck?" he asked. He handed Joe the knife.

Taking it, Joe hefted the handle in his hand, not looking up. It was hard to put it into words. He felt a great bond of sympathy and liking between this middle-aged trainer and himself. It had grown over the years. If anybody could understand him, Joe knew it would be Max Corkle. So he tried to explain, taking a deep breath and looking straight into Max's eyes.

"It's just that it seems I've been working my whole life long to get a chance to do one thing . . . *one thing* . . . and now I don't know if I'm ever gonna get a chance to do it."

Rubbing his aching neck where the stiffness always got him, Max looked hard at Joe. He'd never heard him sound discouraged before, not even when he'd first torn the ligaments in his right knee. He felt a mingling of delight at the precious surprise he was going to spring on Joe, and a pang of sorrow for what sounded like real loneliness in the boy's words. Football . . . it really *was* the kid's life. There really didn't seem to be anything else. Funny, here he was, middle-aged, paunchy, and nowhere, feeling sorry for a great quarterback on his way to more greatness. It didn't figure.

Joe cut a large piece of cake for Corkle. As he handed him the plate, he noticed Max rubbing at his aching neck. Right at the sterno-mastoid muscle. Again! He shook his head.

"Hey, your neck!" Joe got up and started toward Corkle. Alarmed, the older man backed away, holding up one protesting hand.

"Joe . . . no, Joe. It's all right. Really . . . it's okay . . ."

But Joe was coming closer, that certain glint in his eye that Corkle knew so well. The trainer's back was literally against the wall now, and there seemed no way to escape. Joe had caught up with him.

"Come on." Joe was easing behind Max now, reaching around his head to clasp the juncture of the neck firmly.

"Joe . . . Joe . . . easy," begged the apprehensive Max without hope. He closed his eyes and winced.

Joe's hands jerked suddenly, and Max heard a sickening snap.

"There!" Joe cried, triumphant. He let Corkle go. "Better?"

Max rubbed at his neck. It *was* better. That always surprised him. He always expected his head to snap off.

"Yeah, thanks. It always scares the hell out of me when you do that." He sat down on the couch and looked around the living room, marveling again at Joe's simple tastes. His place was comfortable, but nobody could call it luxurious. It was even a little shabby, proof that Joe paid no attention to his surroundings. Football stars generally had Jacuzzis that accommodated four, and hot tubs that seated sixteen. Joe Pendleton had a shower. Hot and cold and that was that.

"I'm telling you." Joe was lecturing Max again, maybe for the thirtieth time this year. "If you don't start paying more attention to the way your trapezius goes into your deltoids, Max, you're gonna throw off your entire cervical and lumbar area. Come on, stand up."

Max cut a large slice of cake for Joe and pushed it at him, shaking his head. "Maybe we oughta change places," he suggested with a smile he couldn't quite suppress. "*You* be the trainer, and *I'll* start on Sunday."

Joe watched in dismay the green and yellow cake coming at him. How could he get out of eating that junk without hurting Max's feelings? That stuff was toxic! You should see what it did to the intestines of laboratory rats. Joe had seen pictures in the health-food magazines that would make the hair on the back of your neck . . . Suddenly, Max's words sank in. Joe

14

could hear them clearly. *You* be the trainer, and *I'll* start on Sunday.

"I'm starting against Dallas?" he asked very quietly.

Now Max allowed the smile to spread into a wide grin. "Yeah. They don't want to go with Jarrett. They want to go with you." He pressed the cake plate into Joe's hands. "Happy birthday, Joe."

A glow of happiness began at Joe's tibialis anterior and worked its way up past the vastus externus to settle in the pectoralis major. With a smile, he lifted a forkful of green and yellow butter cream toxins and shoved it into his mouth. After all, it *was* his birthday cake. One piece might destroy a laboratory rat, but it probably wouldn't be fatal to a starting quarterback.

CHAPTER II

Joe could not remember a happier day, unless it was that time ten years ago when he'd been the Rams' first draft choice. This was a very special day, even though he had planned nothing extraordinary or very special for it. He ran, as usual, he exercised, he swam in the ocean, he played his sax. He did, in short, just about what he'd done every day for months, but he carried around inside him a very special feeling, and it colored the day brighter and infused it with happiness and a sense of his own special history. He was going to start against Dallas. Not only that, the Rams were going to win. He knew it; he could almost taste the victory. He would be getting his chance at last, the big one after ten long years of working for it, waiting for it. The Super Bowl. First Dallas, then the Super Bowl. Oh, yes, it was going to happen.

He spent the day alone, as he preferred. After his morning exercise, he'd pedaled his bike down the dry creek bed of the canyon, looking sadly at the edges of the land crumbling away. Someday the long-overdue rains would finally come, and then this thirsty land would turn into a sea of mud and slide right down, all over those five-hundred-thousand-dollar homes. It was one of the dangers of living in California. That and the fault. Joe hoped California would last out his time; he loved it so much. Today, especially, he was filled with love, for every thing and every place and everybody.

He stopped at a bend of the creek, where the Pacific below came glinting through the eucalyptus, bright and beckoning. There he got off his bike and sat with his back against a tree, quietly playing his saxophone. A man and his music. That was how he liked to think about it. A man and his music. "Louise," maybe. Right? Every little breeze seems to whisper Louise . . . right. Oh, he knew that whenever he played his sax around others, which wasn't often, teeth would be gritted and jaw muscles would tighten and jump. But somehow Joe himself never heard the sour notes. In his head, the music was beautiful, magical, winding, and mysterious, the soprano wail of longing, love and longing. He took his saxophone with him everywhere; how could a man be separated from his music?

After "Louise," he tried "Ticket to Ride" for the first time. It needed working on, but it had possibilities. Then he drank his lunch from a thermos—carrot and cress juice—and ate a couple of whole wheat sesame wafers. After a fifteen-minute nap, he got back on his bike and pedaled down to Malibu, to the ocean. He rode for several miles past Malibu colony, where the most expensive shorefront real estate in the world offered up houses crammed so close together that you could read your next-door neighbor's newspaper over his shoulder as you both sat out on your "private" decks. They say that those whom the gods love have a house in Madrid. In Hollywood, the gods love those who have an A-frame in Malibu. But to Joe, the gods love those who pitched a canvas tent on a deserted beach and didn't leave any cola cans or empty cigarette packs behind, only footprints.

When he came to a deserted part of the beach, he stripped off his gray hooded sweatshirt and his sweatpants, and stood in his swimming trunks, welcoming the early sunshine onto his body. Vitamin D. Alone on the sand, silhouetted against the gently curling tide and the limitless ocean, Joe Pendelton was magnificent. Tall, strong, lithe, handsome in a boyish way, Joe was the closest thing to a natural man that most people would ever see. He didn't talk much, but he knew how to listen. He never lied, because he saw no reason to lie. What was wrong with the truth? He considered the human body a precious gift that had to be treated with responsibility; the spirit he never gave much thought to. It was there or it wasn't; either way, there was nothing much Joe needed to do about it. He was so straight, so totally honest, that a lot of people found him a kook. Joe Pendleton didn't care. Give him his privacy, his music, a healthy body, and the chance to play football, and he was a totally contented man.

Running forward, he threw himself into the ocean and swam out as far as the third wave. There he spent close to an hour, alternately floating and swimming hard against the swells, feeling the effort in his shoulders, neck, and chest muscles, feeling his legs cut cleanly through the water. Then, tired and happy, he lay on the beach and let the sun soak the aches and the kinks out of his body. He lay so still that if you passed this tall young man on the old khaki blanket, you would have thought he was sleeping.

But Joe wasn't asleep. He was working. He lay in the sun running plays in his head, over and over. He remembered every fact he'd ever learned about the Dallas defense, all its strengths and its most recent weaknesses. Who would they field? What would be the team's strategies? He worked them out in his head in every possible combination, delving deeper and deeper into the permutations of play until he *became* the Dallas Cowboys. Now he, Joe Pendleton, was the enemy. How could he best defend himself against the Rams' quarterback? Zone or man to man? He concentrated fiercely on seeing next Sunday's game through Dallas eyes. The hours passed, but Joe didn't heed the time. This was what he needed, these hours of unbroken concentration, the opportunity to map his strategies, plan his plays, and sharpen his instincts. He felt ready now, readier, maybe, than he'd ever been in his life before. And he was hungry for victory, for the applause and the cheer-

ing, the acclamation by his own team, the acknowl-
edgment by the losers. He was ready to show them all.

Suddenly, Joe shivered. The skin on the nape of his
neck prickled. Something . . . what . . . no. The sun
was going down, that was all. It was getting chilly, and
soon it would be getting dark. He stood up and slipped
into his clothing, shook out the blanket, grabbed up
the sax, and repacked his bicycle. The dusk was beginning to settle, stealing in over the ocean, the sky
all pinks and purples, like a Maxfield Parrish print.
The beauty of the sky and the stilling grandeur of the
sea made Joe stop for a moment and draw his breath.
The world was a wonderful place. And life could be
good, very, very good.

Where the past and the future come together, that
is the present, and the present is the only surface on
which we mortals travel. Some of us will go chasing
after our destiny, some will try to evade it. But destiny
is shaped by such tiny little accidents, such impercepti-
ble breaks in the threads that make up the fabric of
life, that no living person can discern the pattern until
long, long afterward. Factors which are out of our
control, about which we can know nothing, can shape
and alter our lives forever. A lunch date broken, a
train missed, and an entirely alternate destiny begins
to take shape. Afterward, if you think hard about it, we
can discover the first innocent, ignorant step that led
us to where we are right now, but we can never tell
where we will be a year from now. Destiny picks its
own time to catch up with us.

Take the case of Joe Pendleton, starting quarterback
for the Los Angeles Rams. Watch him as he pedals
home from the beach, up the winding roadway to the
canyon in the hills. See the things he cannot see, the
strange confluence of factors that are shaping this man's
destiny this very minute.

First, the tunnel in the hills. Just an ordinary tunnel
carved through the mountain some thirty-five years
ago so that automobiles could go through and not

around or over the mountain. A timesaver, but it's dark. Not a long tunnel, not a large tunnel, but a dark tunnel. Cars go in and cars come out.

Next, consider that Joe ordinarily doesn't bike on the roads where the cars go. It's his custom to keep to the dry creek bed or the fire-trails; the exercise is better and it's safer. But this evening he stayed at the beach longer than usual, and he's hungry and eager to get home and look at football movies. So he's biking *on* the road, not alongside it.

Here's another unknown factor. There's a camper on the road. Not one of those cruising Winnebago behemoths, a six-room house on wheels, but a modest camper that moderate people in their forties buy when they leave the Midwest to take a look at California. It has Wisconsin plates, it hugs the middle of its lane, and it obeys the speed laws always. It's obeying them now, doing thirty-five, and sitting right in the middle, chugging along nicely with curtains on the windows and stickers from Disney World and Grand Canyon, Las Vegas and Yosemite, plastered on the back above the license plate. Nice people are inside, and they mean no harm to anybody.

And now see this. Behind the camper is a battered old Ford van covered wtih dayglo decals in the shape of huge daisies. There are kids in the van, surfers. Their expensive fiberglass boards are strapped to the roof, and they're in a hurry. Surf's up; they want to get to the beach within the next five minutes, to hurl their golden young bodies into the darkening water. Who can tell which wave is coming even now all the way from Hawaii, maybe even Japan . . . the wave that will be theirs, the wave to ride all the way to heaven. It's getting late, and they've been real mellow between the beer and the grass. But now they itch for the ocean, and the only thing between them and the wave from Hawaii, maybe even Japan, is that slowpoke old camper smack ahead of them. Pass it, Charlie, come on, man, leave it behind. Hey, no way, not on a curve.

Hey, hurry, man, we're missing the *waves!* Wait, can't ya, until we get to some flat ground? I'll pass it, don't worry. Keep your cutoffs on. And give me a toke.

They are nice people, too, these kids. And they mean no harm to anybody, either.

So there it is: destiny in the form of an old van with dayglo daisies all over it, and a dark tunnel, and a bunch of kids anxious to get to the beach in time for the big one. And a camper that won't get out of the way. And a dark tunnel.

And a man on a bicycle pedaling up from the beach, entering the tunnel at one end just as the van, with no lights, pulls out ahead of the camper at the other end. Destiny.

Better not look; it may be very messy. And cover your ears, because the noise is going to be terrible. Possibly the worst sound you can hear is the crunching noise a body makes when several tons of metal hit it head-on. And the ripping of metal is no symphony, either. It makes the head ache with its clangor and the teeth stand on edge.

Nobody in the cars was injured. The surfboards were smashed to bits, though. And Joe Pendleton didn't have a chance.

What a weird dream. Joe felt . . . he wasn't sure . . . somehow weightless. As if he weren't solid. His feet didn't feel as if they were touching ground. He looked down. They weren't. The sneakers were lost in a kind of white mist. There was mist all around him, but fluffy, not damp. More like clouds. That's it; he was walking on clouds. Of course. Dreams tell the truth, right? And he was happy about next Sunday, starting against Dallas. So his dream was telling him that. The old expression, walking on clouds. Still, he felt funny, and instinctively he tightened his grip on his saxophone. He was wearing his usual exercise outfit, the gray sweatshirt and pants. He carried only his saxophone. He was wearing his watch. He pressed the button and the digital numbers read out. Strange. That was the same time he had a few minutes ago, before the dream, when he was on the bicycle. Five-forty-three.

And he wasn't alone, either. He was dreaming that a little guy was walking next to him, a bank teller, maybe, or an accountant. Yeah, he looked like an accountant in his plain gray flannel suit and black knitted tie, a little plain gray guy in glasses. Was the dream telling him they'd win the Super Bowl and the Rams would all get rich, and would Joe need an accountant for the first time? He pressed his watch again and checked the red digits. Five-forty-three.

"Hey, my watch stopped. It keeps flashing the same time." A weird dream. Because if a digital watch stopped working, it wouldn't flash at all. How did you interpret that?

The little man didn't speak. He walked quietly by Joe's side, almost as if he thought he belonged there.

"I'm dreaming," said Joe. Up ahead he could see something now, and it seemed as if they were moving toward it. Joe recognized the outline as the clouds parted around it. An airplane. It was a large airliner, a DC-10 type, but there were no markings on the side. What airline was it supposed to be? There was one of those airport ladders there, the kind that roll up to the plane, and the passengers were moving up the steps and into the plane, one at a time, silently, without pushing, staying in line. Very dreamlike.

"This is an airplane dream," said Joe. "I forget what they're supposed to mean. They're a good sign, aren't they?" He turned to the little man, who was trying to keep pace with him as they approached the plane. But the little man neither turned his head nor answered, he just plodded along doggedly on Joe's heels.

Now Joe was curious about the plane and he lengthened his stride, leaving the smaller man behind.

"Mr. Pendleton. Mr. Pendleton!" the gray man protested.

Joe was beginning to enjoy this dream. He loved traveling; he never felt uncomfortable in strange towns during the away games. There was always a health-food restaurant somewhere. And he loved airplanes because he enjoyed moving fast.

A long line of people was still waiting to board the plane. They moved slowly forward, their empty eyes staring straight ahead of them. Not turning their heads, not looking at one another, not speaking, they kept the line moving. Joe felt sorry for them; they didn't look as if they were having any fun. He felt a little responsible. After all, it was *his* dream. Wasn't he something like a host?

"Hiya, how ya doing?" Joe grinned cheerfully at a nice-looking old lady. But she didn't grin back. She didn't even look his way.

"How ya doing?" He went down the line a few. No answer.

"You wanna hear a little music?" A host had his duties, and one of them was the entertainment of his guests. Joe lifted the sax to his lips. Maybe "Raindrops Keep Fallin' on My Head" would cheer these folks up a little. Their faces looked so empty, their eyes so vacant.

"No. You'll have to wait in line, Mr. Pendleton." The little gray man had a firm hold on Joe's elbow now and was tugging him back down the line of boarding passengers to the end.

What the heck was this? "This is my dream, isn't it?" demanded Joe. Wait on lines? Stuff lines! He backed away and raised the sax again.

"Mr. Pendleton. You *mustn't* get out of line! Really!" The man's voice and manners were as gray and prissy as his suit. Joe was getting tired of this dream. It was boring, and he suddenly decided that there was no way the airplane trip would be any more interesting.

Now the prissy gray man was approaching the plane, where another gray man stood, holding a clipboard in his hand. As each passenger boarded, the man with the clipboard would check off one more name. Joe didn't like the look of any of this; he wanted to wake up. That's it. He would tell the prissy little man that he wasn't going to take the magical mystery tour; instead, he was going to wake up and watch some more football footage. He had a new line on the Cowboys' second-best ground-gainer that he wanted to think out more clearly.

"Hi," he said to the little gray man.

Exasperation puckered the prissy little mouth and furrowed the nervous little brow. The little head shook negatively.

"Mr. Pendleton," he sighed, "you *cannot* board before your turn."

Joe put up his hands, fingers spread, the sax dangling. "Hey, look. I don't need a turn. I just want to tell you that I'm not getting on that thing." He smiled and started to move away. But the little man was somehow standing in front of him. He moved pretty fast when he wanted to, Joe thought.

"I don't think you quite understand." The little gray man was speaking very firmly. "This is not your ultimate destination. This is a Way Station." He pointed to the airliner. "*That* will take you to your ultimate destination."

Joe shook his head amiably. "That's okay. I'm not going to my ultimate destination," he pointed out. "I'm just gonna do a little runnin' around here until I wake up." He was curious to see what sprinting on dream clouds would feel like.

"Mr. Pendleton," said the fussy little man, frowning, "I'm afraid I have not properly explained to you the basis on which this system operates." He spoke very soberly, very earnestly, looking directly at the startled Joe. "The rules of this Way Station derive from your own. They are the product of your own image and the image of those who share your image. And if you violate the rules, if you question the unifying principles, you violate the rules and principles that govern your own vision of existence. Be warned, Mr. Pendleton, you cannot change the rules of an order without destroying the order. Your own order, Mr. Pendleton, not ours. Our existence is confirmed by the vision of many. Not as many as before the turn of the century, perhaps, but enough still to be here. Your existence, Mr. Pendleton, is a reflection only of yourself. Question that image, and it will no longer exist. Disobey the rules it is comprised of, and you will shatter its core. You will fragment your being, Mr. Pendleton. Your own essential self." The little man looked hard at Joe to see what effect his words were having.

Joe smiled at him, glowing with pride. Although he hadn't understood a word of that whole rap, he was thrilled at the thought that he could dream such high-sounding philosophy. You've got more in your subconscious than I gave you credit for, Joe boy, he told himself. That was pretty deep.

"Hold this, will you?" Joe handed his precious saxophone to the astonished man. "I wanna show you a trick. I only do this once in a while, just to keep my abductor pollicus limber so I don't have a lot of patter with it." Fishing in his pocket, Joe pulled out a coin. "Look carefully. This is a thumb palm. Notice that I have a fifty-cent piece right here." He pressed it on the little gray man. "You want to feel that? I put this perfectly ordinary fifty-cent piece in this hand, say magic words . . . abracadabra . . . and . . . presto!" Joe opened his hand; it was empty. The coin had vanished. "It's gone. You probably think I still have it, but you're wrong, because . . ."

Reaching behind the little man's ear, Joe produced the half dollar with a flourish. "I see it coming out of your ear," he finished on a note of triumph, laughing at the astonished expression on the other man's face.

"That's the only trick I know," he said, retrieving

his precious saxophone. Then he jogged off, enjoying the springy feel of the clouds under his running shoes.

"Mr. Pendleton! Mr. Pendleton!" bleated the little gray man, but Joe pretended not to hear him.

"Gentlemen," said a voice sternly. It came from nowhere. "Gentlemen, what is the delay?"

The little gray man, the Escort, looked up nervously and spoke into nowhere. "Well . . . uh . . . we have received a new arrival who refuses to board."

"That's impossible," snapped the voice. "You have explained the rules to him?"

"Yes, sir," quavered the Escort. His glasses were beginning to fog up, and he longed to wipe them with his pocket handkerchief, but he did not dare.

"Quite clearly?" Annoyance was evident in the clipped phrase.

"Yes, sir." The Escort's collar was suddenly wilting.

"And what was his rebuttal?"

"He took a coin out of my ear," said the Escort in a very small voice.

"Did he?" A touch of amusement crept into the voice. "Perhaps I should have a word with him."

The Escort pointed in the direction that Joe had joggingly taken, and set off to follow him. Behind him came Mr. Jordan himself. Joe hadn't gone far, because there was not far to go. Although he didn't know it, the Way Station was, if anything, circular, and it began and ended without beginning or end. So Joe was easily found. He was still jogging. Even if he was waiting to wake up, he didn't like to see time pass without its being put to good use. Every second between now and next Sunday's game counted double.

"Mr. Pendleton! Mr. Pendleton!"

It was the little gray man again. Joe waved at him affably. "How ya doing?" he asked.

There was another man with him, quite a different breed of cat. This man was impressive, with very dark, piercing, intelligent eyes and a deep, resonant voice. His shoulders were wide and square-set and he looked

27

taller than he was. His hair was a distinguished gray, and thick; it waved over his brow. Joe had seen guys like this before. They were always bosses or owners, and when they talked, you listened.

"Mr. Pendleton," said Mr. Jordan gently, "you know where you are, don't you?"

Joe had stopped jogging and was now running in place. He was getting a little winded. It was time he woke up.

"Call me Joe. Yeah. I'm in the middle of a really weird dream. No offense. This is the weirdest dream I ever had."

The Escort shrugged his gray flannel shoulders. "You see the problem," he told Mr. Jordan.

"Joe? Come here." Although Mr. Jordan's voice was still low-pitched and gentle, Joe found himself obeying without question. He found himself facing that handsome, lined, ageless face and looking into those dark expressive eyes, which looked deeply into Joe's blue ones with a kindly yet imperative expression.

"Joe?"

"Yeah?"

"Joe, I want you to look at me and listen very carefully to what I'm saying."

Joe found himself nodding.

"This is not a dream," continued Mr. Jordan. "Life has a special quality all its own . . . a special feeling . . . and so do dreams. But for you all that is finished. I'm sure you are aware of that, and that you'll take your place with the others." He smiled.

For the first time, Joe Pendleton had an inkling of what the little gray man had been driving at. Way Station . . . waiting his turn on line . . . boarding the plane . . . the unmarked plane . . . the empty eyes of the people on line . . . their silence . . . it was all beginning to fall into place. Joe's mind flashed suddenly on the tunnel. Oh, no! What a crazy dream. Oh, no. No.

But Mr. Jordan's eyes were saying yes.

The smile faded from Joe's face. "Wait a minute . . . just a minute here! Are you trying to tell me that . . . that . . . ?"

Mr. Jordan's eyes said yes.

"Oh, no!" yelled Joe vehemently. "No." He shook his head decisively. "I'm not supposed to be here," he said with conviction.

"But you are here, Joe," Mr. Jordan pointed out softly.

A stubborn look entered Joe's eyes. "Well, then, you guys made a mistake."

The Escort gasped, horrified. "This is really insupportable!" he squeaked. "You're speaking to Mr. Jordan!"

Joe was willing to be reasonable. "Well, anybody can make a mistake," he argued. He knew he was right. He *felt* right. He didn't feel dead. He didn't look like those zombies boarding the airplane. He wasn't supposed to be dead, he was supposed to be starting against Dallas next Sunday. They were just going to have to take his word for it.

The man with the clipboard was at Mr. Jordan's elbow now, looking anxious. "Uh . . . Mr. Jordan . . . we're due to take off pretty soon . . ." he hinted.

Mr. Jordan waved him away with an impatient, impeccable hand. "Yes, I know. I have the situation in hand." He turned to Joe, and a little of the gentleness in his tone was replaced by an edge of austerity. "Joe, if you don't take your place with the others, they won't be able to complete their journey. Do you think that's quite fair?"

"I'm not supposed to be fair," Joe retorted, shaking his head stubbornly. "If this really is heaven, *you're* supposed to be fair. *I* didn't make the mistake." Boy, he really liked that tie Mr. Jordan had on. If he ever wore ties, which he didn't, he'd like one like that. As soon as he got back down to earth, maybe he'd find himself one like it, and even wear it. It was classy.

Now the Escort broke in officiously. "This is *not* heaven—this is a Way Station, and there *is* no mistake."

But Joe knew better. He wasn't going to stand around arguing with officials on his exercise time. These clouds were springier than the artificial turf in the stadium. His knees felt wonderful, and Joe figured that, since he'd be out of here pretty soon, he might as well get in all the jogging time he could. He waved his saxophone at Mr. Jordan and ran off, lifting his knees high as he jogged.

Mr. Jordan stood looking after him thoughtfully. He wasn't satisfied. Certain things . . . little things, but significant . . . were bothering him. They didn't fit the pattern. They didn't fit the *rules*. First, the saxophone. Personal property was forbidden up here, even in the Way Station. All of that was automatically left behind when a soul Crossed Over. Yet Joe was still clutching that shiny gold-colored soprano sax. Wrong. And the coin trick, with the fifty-cent piece. Of all the things that one couldn't take with one, money was the first. Money never came Up. There was nothing spiritual about fifty cents, it was purely temporal and earthbound. Yet Mr. Jordan didn't doubt that Joe Pendleton had pulled one out from behind the Escort's ear. It was the oldest trick in the world. In the universe, actually.

But even the sax and the coin were not what troubled Mr. Jordan the most. No, what had really shaken him were Joe Pendleton's eyes. They were large, blue, lively. That was the word. *Lively* . . . filled with *life*. They were not the eyes of a soul who had Crossed Over. In his thousands of years of experience, Mr. Jordan had seen sparks of life in others' eyes; some people clung to their earthly life with such fierceness that pieces of that fire still remained by the time they reached the Way Station. But they faded fast. Joe's fire was raging full, and showed no sign of fading. Mr. Jordan had seen the eyes of spiritual souls who had left the body gladly to seek their true home Elsewhere. There was a glow in those eyes; they were not fiery, but they glowed. Yet it was an ethereal glow. Not Joe's. Joe Pendleton's eyes burned with the fire of earthly life. They were mortal. They lived.

Mr. Jordan reached a decision. "I want a checkout on Joseph Pendleton," he called. "When is he due to arrive at this Way Station?"

The Escort was dumbfounded. This was totally unprecedented. "Sir . . . what . . . ?" he stammered as Joe, catching the drift, came trotting back.

"The likelihood of one individual being right increases in direct ratio to the intensity with which others try to prove him wrong," Mr. Jordan informed him. He was tense, awaiting the data he'd requested.

The man with the clipboard came up with the printout. " 'Pendleton, Joseph,' " he read aloud. " 'Due to arrive at ten-seventeen A.M., March twentieth of the year two thousand twenty-five.' "

Joe grinned. All *right!* Now let's get the ball rolling. He was getting hungry; it must be well past his dinnertime. There didn't seem to be any clocks here in eternity, and his watch still read five-forty-three, but his stomach could tell time pretty well. He'd been here a long while, it was saying, and he was ready to go home now.

"I don't understand it!" the Escort was gasping as Joe trotted up. "I don't believe it! It can't be! Why, I took him out just before the accident. There's no way that car could have missed him."

Jordan wheeled instantly, his handsome face icy with rage. "You did *what?* You took him *out?* You're not supposed to take him out *before*. You're supposed to wait for the *Outcome*." He regarded the Escort with mingled anger and dismay.

The gray little man looked down in humiliation. He was so embarrassed he wanted to sink down through the clouds. Then he looked up at Mr. Jordan, his

31

eyes pleading. "Yes, I know," he said very softly. "But I was . . . so sure. And it looked as if it was going to be so painful."

Joe felt sorry for the little guy. He had meant well.

"Is this your first assignment as an Escort?" Mr. Jordan asked coldly. He didn't appear to be moved by the little man's embarrassment.

"Yes, sir . . . but . . ."

"And you haven't learned the rules of Probability and Outcome?" Mr. Jordan spoke as if addressing a slow child. "Aren't you aware that every life-and-death situation remains a Probability until the Outcome?"

By now Joe felt he had to intervene. Mr. Jordan was coming down pretty hard on a guy who'd taken the field for the first time. You don't get a touchdown the first time you run with the ball. "Look, so he jumped the gun," he wheedled. "So let's just put me back where you found me and let's forget the whole thing. Okay?"

Mr. Jordan turned to the trembling Escort. "This man must be put back into his body at once," he ordered sharply. He was deeply shaken and was trying to hide it. Episodes like this one were utterly disastrous; they shook foundations. They disturbed the very order of Nature and the Universe.

Joe clapped the Escort heartily on the shoulder. This was more like it! Soy steak for dinner, a carob malt, then early to bed. Way to go! He turned to wave at Mr. Jordan, who stood watching them go. "I'll be seeing you in about fifty years," he called. "Thanks, Mr. Jordan." What the hell, no hard feelings, right? As a matter of fact, it had turned out pretty interesting. Like a dream.

Complicated, too. Like a nightmare. The Escort homed in on Joe's body, and that brought them back down, not to the tunnel, not to the hospital, but to a handsome little chapel and a bed of fresh flowers, over which Max Corkle was trying his damnedest not to cry.

"Oh, dear," the Escort whispered apprehensively.

"Hey, Max!" Joe chortled. "Hey, Max, I'm back. Max?"

"He can't hear you, Mr. Pendleton," said the Escort quietly.

Joe looked around him, bewildered. There were all the guys on the team, their faces serious and sad. They stood around the outside of the chapel—Jarrett, Judson, Figarello; even Bradley, the owners' rep, was present and accounted for. It was a funeral, very obviously a funeral, and newsmen were snapping pictures of Corkle as he bent over the little bed of flowers that would mark Joe Pendleton's resting place.

"Joe . . ." whispered Corkle as soon as the service was over and he was sure the others, departing, could not hear him. "Joe, I hope you . . . uh . . . I hope they got the best damn football team in America in heaven, and I hope God makes you first string." He wiped his hand roughly over his eyes and walked quickly away, passing no more than half an inch from Joe himself, who looked after him in astonishment.

Now the cemetery manager came out of his office with a small silver shovel filled with ashes. As Joe and his Escort watched numbly, the ashes were scattered over the bed of flowers. A vagrant breeze carried some of them away.

"Hey," said Joe, suddenly overcome by unquiet. "Hey, where's my body? I gotta get my body back!" He stared without comprehension at the little pile of scattered ashes. "I go up against Dallas next Sunday. I gotta have my body!"

"Oh, dear," said the Escort guiltily.

"Well, look," explained Joe for the tenth time, "I'm startin' against Dallas on Sunday." He thought that if he said it often enough, it would make everything come out all right. He had no other assurance.

"Joe," said Mr. Jordan again with infinite patience, "the body you occupied on earth has been cremated. Destroyed."

It was too much for Joe to accept. There had to be a way out. *Had* to be. It wasn't *his* mistake, was it? These guys had power, didn't they? "Well, uncremate me, that's all," he demanded. Now he was getting mad. "You guys must be able to do *something* right."

The Escort bristled, his feathers ruffling. "Mr. Pendleton, do the words 'you're not being a good sport' mean anything to you?"

Mr. Jordan had only one recourse open to him in the circumstances. "Joe," he said slowly, frowning in concentration, "we can put you into another man's body provided that his death has not yet been discovered."

Joe's lower jaw dropped open. He was dumbfounded. "Are you kidding?" he howled. "You're gonna put me into some other guy's body? After all the hard work I did on this one? Getting it back into shape and all?" He shook his head. "I don't believe it!" He pounded his fist on the desk angrily. "I just got my body back into shape! I musta run a thousand miles! I musta swum the whole Pacific Ocean! *Another guy's body?!?*"

Mr. Jordan shut his eyes. "I see I shall have to take care of this case personally," he whispered.

CHAPTER III

But bodies don't grow on trees, even if you have the special powers of a Mr. Jordan. And especially if you're as picky as Joe Pendleton. Joe kept insisting that only an athlete's body would do, a body in A-one physical condition, one that could start against Dallas on Sunday. It didn't occur to him . . . no, he refused to *allow* it to occur to him that the Joe Pendleton everybody knew and recognized had blown away in the breeze that ruffled a cemetery flower bed. He refused to consider how he was going to get this new, presumably A-one body accepted by his teammates. First things first, and the first thing was the body. Joe was beginning to really hate being disembodied; it was like wearing a suit with no pockets.

He had no sense of time or space any more. He had stopped being hungry, and didn't need sleep. In their quest for a body, it was not that Mr. Jordan and Joe *went* from one place to another . . . they just sort of . . . materialized. Now they were there, now they weren't. It was spooky, and it was getting to Joe.

The first body that Mr. Jordan located was a racing driver whose striped Porsche was entered at Le Mans. The trick was to catch the number just as it was coming up, to slip into the body at the moment its original owner was slipping out—in short, to move in before anybody discovered the vacancy. Joe was troubled on two counts: first, he couldn't get a good look at the driver, who was folded neatly into the tiny machine, and he had never heard that racing

35

drivers were long on muscles. They spent too much time sitting down. Second, as this about-to-be-no-more driver yelled his instructions to his mechanics in the pit stop, Joe was horrified to hear the words come out in German.

"*Schnell! Schnell! Kein entritt doch den machina-farben!*" commanded the driver while the mechanics hopped to.

Joe turned to Mr. Jordan, aghast. "He's not talking English!"

"I told you he was German." Mr. Jordan shrugged.

"Yeah, but I thought—hey!" he shouted suddenly at the driver, who sat scowling while his wheel nuts were being tightened. "Can you speak any English?"

But of course nobody could see or hear Joe, as Mr. Jordan had pointed out more than once.

"I don't want to talk German," said Joe sullenly as the car roared out of the pit and back onto the track, to meet its own personal destiny.

On the other hand, it didn't really matter. It proved to be academic—German or English. The condition of the body, after the impact of the Porsche with the wall at the turn, was such that nobody could ever inhabit it again. Even Joe's ashes were in better condition.

Joe had real hope, briefly, for the swimmer. The swimmer was in good shape, a little top-heavy, perhaps, the legs not long enough to suit Joe completely, but a definite possibility. Joe even felt a little sorry for the guy, having to drown in the middle of a meet that way. Until he saw the swimmer blow a little kiss to his beloved as he stepped into the pool. And the beloved blew a kiss back, right through *bearded lips*. No way. Joe was not coming back into this life as a bowl of cherry Jell-O, not even if the body had belonged to Mark Spitz.

Mr. Jordan shrugged.

The tightrope walker was much too short. His balance and agility, his physical condition, were not in dispute, but he would never be able to see over the line of scrimmage to pick out an unblocked receiver. Scratch the tightrope walker.

Joe was getting desperate. This wasn't as easy as he'd thought it was going to be. Somehow, when they started this search for a body, Joe had envisioned a body exactly like his, to be pulled out of a hat by Mr. Jordan, like a rabbit in a magic show. But not too many men died in the peak of physical condition, in the prime of their lives. Even though Joe and Mr. Jordan were traveling timelessly, on another plane where Joe's watch always flashed five-forty-three, Joe had a sense of time running out. He couldn't wait forever for a new body; sometimes he felt a little funny, as though he himself were beginning to fade.

Even Mr. Jordan was getting edgy. He wanted this matter resolved as quickly as possible so that he could get on with his Eternal duties and Order in the Universe could be restored. Besides, he liked Joe and felt sorry for him, snatched erroneously from life on the eve of his big chance. Joe still thought it would all be simple. Ah, if he only knew . . .

The Big Computer in the Sky had exhausted all the possible athletes in its Celestial Data Bank. It was time to try a compromise. Joe didn't know it, but he was beginning to fade a little, thought Mr. Jordan. He had better be placed inside a body before his outlines dimmed. There was one possibility; not an athlete, but at least a Los Angeles man. The geography was right. And there were other advantages . . .

"What is this place? A museum?" Joe asked curiously as they . . . materialized . . . through the electronically secured wrought iron gates and into the formal gardens around the driveway that led three quarters of a mile up to the house.

"No, it's a private home."

A private home? It looked more like a university, with its pillars and its porticos and its gigantic size. And there were guards, two uniformed private security police, armed, flanking the front door like library lions.

"Hey, private fuzz," marveled Joe, gesturing with his saxophone.

"He's very wealthy," Mr. Jordan told him. "Leo Farnsworth. And he's just about your age."

As they walked up the front steps, Joe craned his neck to admire the dark blue limousine that a uniformed chauffeur was polishing with the best-grade wax. It was a block long, and of a make that Joe didn't recognize, never having laid eyes on a custom-built Daimler before.

They . . . materialized . . . through the mahogany front door with its silver knocker and into an entrance hallway that could have accommodated Joe's entire house in Topanga, with room left over to hold a square dance. A long double staircase stood at the far end of the hall, with curving banisters of polished cherry. The floors were of polished terrazzo marble, and a chandelier of heavy crystal drops, each one scrubbed to a rainbow, hung from the center of the ceiling. Joe had been right. It *was* a museum.

But Mr. Jordan was walking with long, purposeful steps toward an open door at the far end of the foyer. Joe followed, still looking around him curiously. As he passed it, he peeped into a living room that must have been at least forty by eighty. It was filled with polished furniture and shiny fabric; a fire was burning in the fireplace, but nobody was in the room.

A butler was coming out of a little door under the stairs, carrying a tray. Joe froze; he kept forgetting that he was invisible. The butler, unruffled, carried the tray in through the open door, and Mr. Jordan beckoned Joe to follow.

The room was evidently a library. Books lined the walls from floor to ceiling, books bound in leather and arranged in sets by the colors of their bindings. The titles were printed in gold. A tall rolling ladder was fixed to a ladder rail that ran around the top of the solid walnut, glass-fronted bookcases. The ladder looked as if nobody had ever stepped on it to get a book, and the books themselves didn't look as if anybody had ever taken them off the shelves to look inside the leather bindings. The room was small by the standards of the house, no more than twenty by thirty feet. But it was big enough to hold a lot of leather furniture, an antique globe of the world, and two very nervous-looking people, a man and a woman.

"Thank you, Sisk," said the man to the butler as he set the tray, with its crystal decanter of brandy and two balloon snifters, on a small polished table. "And just leave the door open, please."

As the butler departed on silent feet, the man turned to the woman and said, "The more servants who see us, the better it will be."

"Who are they?" Joe asked Mr. Jordan.

"Farnsworth's wife and his confidential secretary."

Wife? Was he going to have a wife? Joe took a closer look. She seemed to be pretty enough, with lots and lots of long blonde hair, but it was a little hard to tell what her face really looked like, because the woman wore so much makeup and her expression now was one of near hysteria. She looked tense enough to crumble at a single touch, like a thin sugar cookie.

"Would you give me a drink, please." Julia Farnsworth spoke shrilly, less a request than a demand.

"Don't drink," replied Leo Farnsworth's confidential secretary. It was less a reply than a command.

"You hate me." Julia's face started to crumble.

"Don't be ridiculous, darling," snapped Tony Abbott. "I don't hate you. I love you. I just don't think that now is the time for you to drink." He was a rather chunky man, dressed in a navy blue blazer that fit him a little too snugly. Like Julia, Tony wore too much gold jewelry. Unlike Julia, he didn't have masses of hair. What he had instead of real hair was a rather obvious rug.

Now Julia Farnsworth was beginning to babble a

little. "We couldn't help it, could we, Tony? We couldn't help it," she squeaked.

"No. Julia, I really would feel better if you didn't unravel now," he said as calmly as he could. He watched her take a deep, choking breath. "Thank you, Julia."

"Is this guy Farnsworth dead yet?" Joe asked Mr. Jordan.

"Not yet."

"Well, maybe I can take a look at him." Joe didn't like this setup at all; it made him extremely uncomfortable to watch these two only mildly attractive people going to pieces. It wasn't going to be worth it. He could tell. This was a situation that didn't appear to have possibilities leading to Dallas on Sunday.

"Just as you wish." Mr. Jordan smiled. Nothing ever bothered him.

Farnsworth was in the bathtub. Joe had once seen a picture of an ancient Roman palace, and Farnsworth's bathroom looked just like it. There was marble everywhere, with solid gold fixtures. The tub iself stood on a raised platform three feet above sea level, and was reached by carpeted steps. Inside the tub, a man lay dying.

Joe looked at him critically. Although the marble tub was big enough for three people, Farnsworth took up a fair amount of room. He was about six feet three inches tall and had a decent physique, although there was a tendency to flab here and there, and none of the muscles had been developed to Joe's satisfaction. Still, the body had good possibilities as a body. Tall, broad-shouldered, long-armed, long-legged . . . the basics were there.

The man's eyes were closing now, and he was slipping deeper and deeper into the steaming, scented bath water.

"He can't even keep his eyes open. What's the matter with him?" asked Joe.

"He's been drugged by those two downstairs," Mr.

Jordan told him. "You see how he's slowly sliding into the water. In a very short time, he'll drown. This is a murder."

A murder! Joe's eyes opened wide; he looked again at the naked drugged figure in the tub. Then he ran out of the bathroom into the adjacent dressing room. It was huge, lined with closets and mirrors on both sides, and papered in marbleized wall coverings to match the real marble of the master bath. There was nobody in the dressing room. The dressing room led on to the master bedroom, where a serious-faced valet was fussing with some clothing, arranging it on the bed and stepping back to get the maximum effect. Joe hurried by him and through Farnsworth's adjacent private study, out into the hall.

A good-looking girl in a maid's uniform was polishing the leaves of a large potted plant on the landing outside the study door. Breathless, Joe yelled at her, "Hey, get a doctor! There's a guy drowning in the bathtub!"

But he couldn't be seen or heard. Another maid, good-looking in a different way, approached the first one. She was carrying two small flower arrangements; a watering can dangled from her left hand.

"You know you left a bare pot on the carpet, Lavinia. Mrs. Farnsworth would be very upset."

"Well, I can't carry everything, Corinne," Lavinia retorted.

Neither one of them could see or hear Joe. He ran down the long flight of stairs and back into the library. Mr. Jordan was already there, a slight smile on his face, waiting for Joe. Joe still didn't fully comprehend Probability and Outcome, he thought.

Joe stared at Tony Abbott and Julia Farnsworth with new interest. Murderers, he thought grimly. Not merely a pair of overdressed weirdos, but genuine murderers. They made his flesh crawl. Well, not his flesh . . . but his spirit.

"They did it, huh?"

Mr. Jordan merely nodded.

"No kidding? They're murderers?"

"I want a drink," Julia demanded childishly, reaching for the brandy decanter.

"Please, Julia." Tony grabbed at her hand.

"They just killed somebody, and now they're standing around talking," Joe marveled. Mr. Jordan didn't appear surprised.

Now Julia, on the edge of hysteria and drinkless, began to pace back and forth like a caged cat. Her gold bracelets clanked with every nervous step. "We did it. I'm glad we did it. I wish he were awake so that he could know what was happening to him," she snarled. Her control was wearing very thin, and it hadn't been fat control to begin with.

"Julia," said Tony warningly, "try not to go overboard."

"He was a sadistic, lecherous son of a bitch," continued his about-to-become widow. "Everybody wanted him dead."

Joe winced. "Can we look for another body?" he asked Mr. Jordan plaintively. He'd almost rather come back as a bowl of cherry Jell-O than as a sadistic, lecherous son of a bitch whom everybody wanted dead.

But Mr. Jordan didn't look a bit perturbed. The gentle smile never left his face as he watched Tony and Julia play out their little scene.

Now Tony came up to Julia and slipped his arms around her shoulders. "Darling, try to act normally," he wheedled.

Julia jumped as if she'd been shot with a bow and arrow. "Normally?" she shrieked, her voice rising. "What's that? How do we behave normally? What's normally?"

She had a point there, thought Joe.

"Oh, darling," Tony murmured into her heavy mane of artificially highlighted hair. "Please don't act like this. I beg of you, Julia, please be the dignified lady I know you can be."

Joe could hear Julia's teeth grinding across the large room. "Dignified lady?" she squeaked, almost unable to talk. "What's that? You *idiot!* Oh, God, I should be canonized!" She threw her hands out in a dramatic gesture, nearly knocking Abbott over.

"Perhaps *one* drink," said Tony hurriedly. As he made a dive for the brandy decanter, the sound of rising voices from the hallway outside claimed his attention. "Sisk!" he yelled. "What's going on out there?"

Joe came up to Mr. Jordan and tugged at his sleeve. "I don't like this. Please let's get out of here. I don't want to be Leo Farnsworth."

But Mr. Jordan merely held up one finger to his lips. Quiet, Joe, said the finger. Watch. Listen.

The butler appeared in the doorway, looking harassed. "I'm sorry, sir. It's that Miss Logan here again, sir, to see Mr. Farnsworth."

"Show her in," commanded Abbott with perfect aplomb, pulling the cuffs of his shirt down.

As soon as the butler had left, Julia swooped down on the brandy decanter. "Oh, my God!" It was half a moan, half a scream, and wholly hysterical.

But Tony was smiling, pleased and enthusiastic. "No, no," he assured her. "It's perfect. A perfect alibi. She'll insist on seeing him." He took the decanter out of her hands and shook her gently by the shoulders. "Excuse yourself when she gets here and keep Sisk with you . . . at all times . . . to establish your whereabouts."

This was really beginning to stink. Joe's desperation was mounting by the minute. *"Please* let's get out of here," he begged. He headed for the door, but Mr. Jordan didn't budge. He just stood there, looking very much at home in a rich man's library. On his face was that same serene smile. Joe stopped, perplexed.

"Ah, Miss Logan," purred Tony Abbott, holding out a plumpish hand with manicured fingernails.

As Sisk led Betty Logan into the library, Joe learned in one split second—the nucleus of eternity—the difference between a pretty girl and a beautiful woman. In one split second his brain registered an image so intense as to leave its imprint there forever.

She was tall . . . no, she was small, actually, but she looked tall, because she was so slender and held herself so straight. She was what Nature must have intended woman to look like when time first dawned on earth. She was the living reason Adam ate the apple. Her hair was a golden mass . . . clouds, yellow clouds. Her mouth was full. Where had lips like that ever been before? It was her eyes, though, that left the imprint on Joe's visual screen. Eyes like the Pacific Ocean, as vast, as limitless. They were blue . . . dark blue. No, they were gray. No, green. Joe could spend a thousand lifetimes happily trying to figure out their color. Without thinking, he took a step forward and held his hand out. He had to touch her. She couldn't see him.

"I'm Tony Abbott," the secretary's oily voice continued. "This is the library. Won't you come in?"

Wordlessly, the young woman shook Abbott's hand briefly and walked with quiet dignity into the library. She was simply dressed in a light wool jacket and skirt, and she wore no jewelry and almost no makeup.

Julia Farnsworth glued a bright smile on her face and greeted Betty Logan without warmth. "I'm going into the living room, Sisk," she said, much too carefully and loudly. "Would you like to come into the living room with me?"

"Certainly, madame," said the puzzled butler. He followed her to the double doors that separated the living room from the library and opened them for Julia. Then he carefully closed them again, behind himself and Julia, leaving Tony and Betty Logan alone. Or what everybody except Joe and Mr. Jordan thought was alone.

"Well," said Tony Abbott brightly as he led the way to a long, highly polished cherrywood desk at the far side of the library. "I'm Mr. Farnsworth's personal, private Executive Secretary. I don't know whether you know that or not. I'm sorry that Mr. Farnsworth isn't down yet."

"I'll wait," said Betty Logan quietly. What an idiot, she thought.

"Would you care to take a seat?"

"No, thank you."

Tony walked around the desk and sank into Leo Farnsworth's personal, private Queen Anne leather swivel chair. He made a gothic steeple of his fingers and tried to look solemn and intelligent. And businesslike. "Perhaps you'd like to tell me what it's about," he said in his best personal, private Executive Secretary tones.

I suppose I have to deal with the flunky before I can get to the master, thought Betty Logan. She took a deep breath. "Mr. Farnsworth has been sent hundreds of letters from a town in England called Pagglesham," she began.

England, thought Joe. That's why she sounds like that. She's English. Her voice was low-pitched and a little husky, and as musical as a mountain stream running over polished stones. To Joe, she sounded like an alto saxophone that never blew a wrong note.

"The people who live in that town," continued Betty with strong conviction, "sixteen hundred, including my father, are about to be forcibly evicted from their homes in order to make way for the proposed Exo-Grey refinery. Not only will hundreds of families who have lived there for generations be forced to find other homes, but those few who remain will have their health endangered by the inevitable poisoning of their air and water, the documented evidence for which I have here . . ." She took off her plain

45

leather shoulder bag and pulled some papers out of it. "Along with a petition . . ." Another paper was added to the sheaf; she held the pile out to Tony Abbott, who reached for it, only to see the papers snatched away and tucked back into the bag.

". . . a petition signed by the sixteen hundred and seventy-three citizens of the area. This is what I'm here to see Mr. Farnsworth about," the girl concluded firmly.

Ah, a radical. One of those loony do-gooders. All the better, thought Abbott. "As I'm sure you know," he said aloud, "Mr. Farnsworth usually conducts business at his office, Miss Logan."

"Yes. I've been to the office. He refused to see me."

Refused to see you? thought Joe. He must be blind as a bat. Who could refuse to see springtime? Who could refuse to see sunshine?

"Then I seriously doubt that he'll see you here," said Tony, enjoying this. This was working out better than he'd dared hope. This hothead would be the best witness he could ask for.

Betty Logan squared her slim, beautiful shoulders. "He'll have to," she said stubbornly. "Because I'm not leaving."

I'll say you're not, thought Abbott. Not until those honest eyes of yours have seen the "accident." "I beg your pardon?" he said, as if his ears were playing tricks on him.

"I said I'm not leaving. I've come eight thousand miles, Mr. Ab—Mr. Abbott," she said, searching for his name, "in order to do something about a terrible injustice that this man—Leo Farnsworth—has perpetrated on hundreds of innocent, defenseless people!" Her eyes flashed with a brilliant fire that turned their depths navy blue.

"Boy, she's really something, isn't she Mr. Jordan?" Joe was forming an admiration for her spirit as well as for the rest of her. He'd never seen a woman like this one before.

"That she is, Joe." Mr. Jordan smiled quietly.

"Mr. Farnsworth is a very, very busy man," Tony was saying pompously.

"Somebody ought to help her," Joe murmured wistfully.

"You can help her, Joe. You can be Farnsworth," said Mr. Jordan. Joe looked startled; the thought had not occurred to him.

"If Mr. Farnsworth doesn't see me, I don't know *what* I'll do," Betty burst out.

"Is that some sort of threat, Miss Logan?" asked Abbott smoothly.

"Yes!" cried Betty. Then she thought about it a second or two. "Well, yes," she added uncertainly.

"Really?" A scornful eyebrow headed upward toward Abbott's toupee.

"Yes," said Betty with certainty. Her chin came up defiantly.

Joe looked helplessly at Mr. Jordan. He was racked by indecision, torn by doubts. On the one hand was his desire to be of service to this strong, beautiful girl. That was so simple. On the other hand, there was the prospect of coming back as a married millionaire who was obviously one of the worst bastards on the planet. And a murdered millionaire, to boot, with the murderers still loose in the house. It was all so complicated.

"I'd like to help her, but I don't want to be Farnsworth," moaned Joe. It was a cry from the heart.

"The decision is yours, Joe." Mr. Jordan was unable to heed that cry. It *had* to be Joe's decision, because it was Joe's destiny. Joe didn't understand that yet, but he would.

"Very well, then, Miss Logan. You leave me no choice." Abbott was saying now. "Sisk!" He raised his voice for the butler.

Joe thought fast. He knew that he stood on a crucial instant in time, and he couldn't drag his feet. This fine young woman was about to be used as an unwitting accomplice in a murder, about to become the tool by which the murderers would escape free and clear. She was going to witness an "accident," and that would be a terrible experience for her in itself.

"Let me ask you this," said Joe quickly to Mr. Jordan. "If I have to be Farnsworth, could we make it temporary?" Without knowing it, he took the first step on the path of his destiny.

"Sisk!" bawled Abbott.

"We can arrange that, if you wish it, Joe," said Mr. Jordan.

Sisk opened the doors that led from the living room to the library. "Yes, sir?"

"Sisk, please tell Mr. Farnsworth that Miss Logan is here and refuses to leave."

"Yes, sir." The butler headed for the stairs and the master bathroom.

"But if you want to help her, Joe, you'll have to hurry."

But Joe hesitated, still caught in a web of uncertainties. "Well . . . it's only temporary, right?"

"That is correct." Mr. Jordan nodded.

"I don't want to be Farnsworth," Joe insisted.

"The moment the body is discovered, it will be too late," Mr. Jordan reminded him gently.

"I don't know." Joe turned to look at Betty again. Her beauty had entranced him, and her plight had caught hold of the gallant knight that lives in the heart of every good man.

"Only Farnsworth can help her," said Mr. Jordan, his keen dark eyes probing Joe's face.

Deciding, Joe nodded.

Upstairs, Mr. Jordan held up the terry-cloth robe while Joe stepped out of the tub and wrapped himself in it. As he rubbed himself dry, he caught a glimpse of his image in the mirrored wall of the vast bathroom. Joe Pendleton's face stared back at him, catching him totally by surprise.

"Hey, it's *me!*" he cried excitedly. He turned to Mr. Jordan. "It's still *me!* I haven't changed! Look!"

Mr. Jordan looked. He saw Leo Farnsworth, not Joe Pendleton. But Farnsworth's face now possessed a pair of vivid blue eyes, Joe's eyes. That's what the world would see. Leo Farnsworth. Now he was looking at Joe again. Joe Pendleton. Only he and Joe could see *that* face, and only because this was a temporary situation.

Joe flexed his shoulder muscles, raised his bare right leg and looked at it, made a fist, and probed his biceps. He had a body again. He wasn't quite sure yet, but he thought it felt wonderful.

CHAPTER IV

"Mr. Farnsworth." Discreet knuckles rapped on the door of the bathroom, and the voice was Sisk's.

"What'll we do?" Joe asked Mr. Jordan, suddenly panic-stricken.

"Mr. Farnsworth. Are you there, sir?"

Joe looked around the bathroom. There was no body in the tub. Joe was standing in the body. "I can't get away with this," he said wildly.

The knocking became more insistent. "Are you all right, Mr. Farnsworth?" The butler was sounding worried, although his words were muffled by the heavy door. "Mr. Farnsworth?" Sisk called again.

"Answer him, Joe," said Mr. Jordan. He was perfectly calm.

Joe looked at him, startled. "You mean people can *hear* me now?"

"Of course."

"But he knows the other guy's voice!" Joe protested.

"Mr. Farnsworth!" Sisk was shouting now and banging on the door. "Is everything all right in there?" Downstairs, Tony Abbott could hear the banging and shouting, and he smiled secretly to himself. Julia Farnsworth caught her breath and held it, looking up at the ceiling in terror.

"Joe. Answer him," ordered Mr. Jordan gently.

"Hey, just take it easy!" called Joe. "I'll be with you in a minute." His palms suddenly felt sweaty.

"Very good, sir," said the butler at once to the closed bathroom door.

51

Startled, Joe sought Mr. Jordan's face for reassurance. "Hey, it works!" he breathed.

Mr. Jordan nodded at him. "Inwardly, you haven't changed," he informed Joe. "You and I will still see Joe Pendleton. Outwardly, it's Leo Farnsworth that other people will see and hear." He gestured at the bathroom door, tilting his head expectantly at Joe. Hesitantly, Joe walked to it, opened it, and went into his dressing room.

Sisk was standing at one of the large wardrobe closets, selecting the correct pair of socks. "Sir," he said at once, "Miss Betty Logan is downstairs. She insists upon seeing you. Do you wish to dress, sir?"

Joe swallowed. It would be difficult for him to accept, but evidently it was true. He *was* Leo Farnsworth; nobody would be able to detect any difference. He hoped. "Uh . . . sure, sure," he told the butler.

"Very good, sir."

But Joe was still insecure. He turned to Mr. Jordan, who stood observing him with evident amusement. "Wait a minute, you mean I'm gonna sound like this guy no matter how I talk?" he demanded.

"I beg your pardon, Mr. Farnsworth?" said the puzzled Sisk.

Joe bit his lip. Now everything he said aloud, even to Mr. Jordan, was audible. What a pain *that* was going to be. As long as it was only temporary . . .

The other guy in the bedroom was coming up now, holding out silk underwear for Farnsworth to step into. What the hell? A valet, right? Couldn't this guy dress himself without help? He wasn't gonna let any guy help him on with his underwear, not Joe Pendleton, not if he were crippled in both legs. With a look of helpless terror, Joe backed away from Bentley, shaking his head. Mr. Jordan smiled.

Excusing himself to Betty Logan, Tony Abbott walked swiftly into the living room and closed the doors carefully and firmly behind himself. By now it should be all over; he was only waiting for a scream

from Sisk. But Julia still worried him. She really had
the most fragile nature; if he didn't take a firm hand
with her, she'd go to pieces in front of witnesses, and
it would all be over before they got a chance to spend
the money. He'd better check on her.

Aha. Not a moment too soon. She was filling up
her glass again. Abbott loped heavily across the length
of the living room and wrestled the decanter out of
Julia's trembling fingers. She had to let the bottle go,
but she made a grab for the glass.

"One more sip," she begged, rolling her eyes wildly.
Her hair was straggling into her face, and she looked
guilty enough for a hanging.

"Darling, not now," said Tony through clenched
teeth. Snatching the glass away from her, he made a
feeble attempt to pat her hair into shape with his
fingers. "Julia, listen to me, dear—"

"You're sorry to have me, aren't you?" Julia interrupted in a strangled voice. "You wish he were alive,
don't you? You hate me!" she accused hysterically.

Abbott sighed loudly and cast his eyes up to heaven.
"Julia . . . *please*. Not now!"

"Then why didn't you say it's not true? You didn't
say it's not true." Tears were trembling on the edges
of Julia's mascara.

"Julia, it's not true," Tony assured her. He pushed
her gently down on the couch and perched on the arm.
"It's not true. Be calm, dear. It's only a matter of
another minute or two. You must hold yourself together until it's all over."

Joe stared at himself in the mirror, incredulous.
He looked as if he were on his way to a costume
party, but he had no idea what he was going as. They
had dressed him for polo. Honest to God, polo. He
wore a polo shirt of white cotton, tucked neatly into
polo jodhpurs of white twill, which were tucked in
turn into tall, gleaming polo boots. The pants and
the shirt were separated by a wide polo belt that

matched the leather of the boots and fastened with three straps, cinching the waist tightly. Around Joe's neck was carelessly flung a long white silk polo scarf. All he needed was the horse—oops, pony. He felt like a horse—oops, horse's ass.

And it had taken two men to dress him, too, buckling his belt and pulling on his boots as if Joe were a baby. No, Farnsworth, he corrected himself. This was evidently the way Farnsworth liked things. Maybe millionaires never dressed themselves. Too busy earning interest.

Sisk now stepped up behind Joe and lovingly draped a camel-colored, double-breasted, belted cashmere coat over his shoulders, stepping back to observe the effect. It was, of course, a polo coat. For inside the house. A coat.

Bentley was rummaging around in the closet, and now he emerged with a white helmet, which he handed to Sisk. Sisk in turn passed it on to Farnsworth.

"Your helmet, sir?"

Joe stared at it blankly. Helmet meant football helmet, and this overripe thing was no football helmet. "What?"

"Your polo helmet, sir."

Joe shook his head slightly, dazed. "Do I play polo?" he inquired.

"No, sir, not really," said the imperturbable Sisk.

"Ah. Right." Joe took the helmet and clapped it on his head, turning to find Bentley holding out a polo mallet. Automatically, Joe accepted it. He stood there, clad from ears to toes in his polo gear. What the well-dressed man will wear to a meeting in his library. The horse's-ass feeling deepened and spread. But if this was Farnsworth's life-style . . . Joe shrugged, and followed Sisk out of the master bedroom and onto the landing, down the stairs and into his new life as Leo Farnsworth.

"Miss Logan, sir," announced Sisk as he swung the library doors open.

"Hi. How ya doing?" Joe asked the extraordinary young woman with eyes like the Pacific Ocean.

"I'm not leaving until you've heard what I've come all this way to tell you . . ." Betty began indignantly, then stopped as the full impact of Joe's magnificent costume washed over her. What a horse's ass, she thought. He's dressed for a chukka; no, for an entire *month* of chukkas. She had to bite her lips to keep from laughing out loud.

"Okay," said Joe uncomfortably, leaning his polo mallet against a library chair and hoping it wouldn't fall. "That's good."

"Have you read the letters?" demanded Betty, frowning earnestly at him. God she was pretty when she frowned.

Letters. What letters? Joe glanced over at Mr. Jordan for help, but Mr. Jordan just shrugged slightly and spread his hands. Joe looked at Sisk. Sisk stared back blankly.

"Uh . . . letters . . . well, no . . . I haven't . . ."

Betty Logan raised one vindicated eyebrow. "You haven't read them," she said flatly. "I suspected as much. That's why I've flown over here, eight thousand miles."

Sisk withdrew discreetly, closing the library doors after him.

Now Betty Logan was rummaging in her shoulder bag for her papers. "Mr. Farnsworth, I and the sixteen hundred and seventy-three people whom I represent and whose names are on this petition . . ." She held the papers out to Joe, who accepted them gingerly, his eyes never leaving her face.

". . . are not going to allow their futures to be determined by a pack of mindless bureaucrats at the beck and call of certain so-called industrialists like yourself for whom elderly men and women and, I might add, children are just so many figures to be entered in the profit-and-loss columns of your accountants' ledgers." At this point she ran out of breath and paused for a moment. Joe, still staring at her, dropped the coat off his shoulders and attempted to disentangle himself from the long scarf while still clutching at the papers.

"Am I making myself clear?" Betty demanded.

"Well . . . yeah . . . but . . ."

"There are no 'buts,' Mr. Farnsworth," the girl interrupted firmly. "You can, of course, call your armed guards and have me dragged out, but if you do, it will be very bad publicity for Exo-Grey Industries, and I don't think the stockholders would like that."

A flush had risen in her cheeks, turning them pink, and her indignation gave her hair and skin an aura of energy. Joe had never seen anybody quite as vital as this slight young woman who stood before him breathing heavily with anger, her thin nostrils flaring.

"No," admitted Joe, "I guess they wouldn't. Now, why don't you sit down?" He smiled and pulled a chair out for himself.

"I prefer to stand," said Betty frostily.

Caught in mid-sit, Joe jumped to his feet on the instant. "Okay, you can stand, then."

What a strange man, thought Betty. He seemed uncomfortable in his own skin. And he had the warmest, most intense blue eyes. They didn't seem to go with the rest of him. "Mr. Farnsworth," she began again, "I have made it my business to find out all I can about Exo-Grey Industries. A lot of facts that would make very interesting newspaper copy," she threatened.

"Yeah?" Joe said with interest. "I'd like to hear them."

The door to the hallway opened suddenly as Sisk entered in all his butler majesty, followed by a footman rolling a large, heavy cart loaded down with silver. "Your tea, Mr. Farnsworth," he announced in round tones.

"My . . . uh . . . what?" asked Joe, taken by surprise.

He glanced over at Mr. Jordan, who nodded to him. "Oh, er, yes, my tea."

Everett, the footman, wheeled the cart over to Joe, who was thus forced to sit down abruptly behind it.

"Will there be anything else, Mr. Farnsworth?"

Who was *this* guy? How many more servants were there whose names he didn't know?

"No, I think that's it," Joe told the footman. "Uh, thanks a lot."

He *was* peculiar, thought Betty Logan as she watched Leo Farnsworth closely. Thanking the servants! She supposed it was what being nouveau riche was all about, not knowing how to behave or—another glance at the polo outfit—how to dress. They knew how to serve, though. At least somebody did. Mrs. Farnsworth, perhaps? Betty eyed the tea cart a little angrily. Talk about cultural rape by barbarians! The tea service was solid silver, and late Georgian. Part of *my* heritage, not Farnsworth's, thought Betty. Not bloody likely Farnsworth's. A tea service like that, with its tall, graceful hot-water urn, its delicate silver dish of paper-thin lemon slices, its ebony-topped teapot and charming little cream jug, belonged in a museum for everyone to enjoy, not merely to be at the disposal of one selfish American millionaire.

Joe looked miserably at the complicated set of silver jugs, pitchers, and urns. To him, "tea" meant a teabag filled with Mu or Red Zinger and some hot water. Which of these doohickeys held the tea?

"You want some tea?" he asked Betty bleakly.

"I *want* to know what you're going to do about Pagglesham," Betty demanded pointedly.

"About what?" Joe did not understand the question.

"Pagglesham," repeated Betty Logan through clenched lips.

"Pagglesham?" echoed Joe blankly. What the hell was a paggel shum? Wait . . . right! Now he remembered. It was a place in England.

"Pagglesham! *Pagglesham!*" yelled Betty, losing her temper. "It's what we've been talking about! Mr. Farnsworth, these people care very much that their community doesn't become yet another one destroyed in the name of free enterprise." Her cheeks were pink again, with earnestness, and her eyes had changed color to gray. Joe pushed the tea trolley away and stood up so that he could see her better when she talked. She was something to see, all right, as she punctuated her words with expressive gestures of her small, very feminine hands. He was happy to notice that she wore no rings, especially not on her left hand. But he paid attention to what she was saying, too. Hadn't he become Farnsworth—temporarily, of course —especially to help her?

"Oh." Joe nodded his comprehension. "That's Pagglesham. I get it. Well, it sounds like a really nice place."

Betty Logan eyed him with suspicion. She knew evasive tactics when she heard them, and this Leo Farnsworth appeared to be a master of evasion. "Mr. Farnsworth, these people are not going to allow you to intimidate and frighten them," she said with a toss of her beautiful curly head.

"Listen, Miss Logan . . . I don't frighten anybody. Believe me—"

It was rather poor timing for that statement, since at that very instant the connecting doors to the library were flung open, and Julia Farnsworth, taking one look at the walking, talking body of her husband, began screaming her head off.

Tony Abbott, his face chalk-white, clapped his hand firmly over Julia's mouth, cutting her off in mid-scream, and dragged her back into the living room. Betty and Joe could hear a whole new series of screams coming through the closed doors, until they, too, stopped abruptly.

"What in God's name was that?" asked Betty, scared half to death.

"That . . . uh . . . that was my . . . uh . . ."
Choking on the word "wife," Joe managed to finish
with "Uh . . . my Mrs. Farnsworth." She just saw
a ghost, Joe wanted to tell Betty, but he knew it would
be a mistake. Mr. Jordan was watching him closely,
one eyebrow raised.

Suddenly, some measure of reality washed over Joe.
What had he gotten himself into? Here he was, a
living ghost, trapped in the same house as his would-be
murderers. All because of a small, thin English girl
with frizzy hair and very large eyes. What a mess!

Having pulled, pushed, and dragged the screaming
Julia across a living room as long as the *Queen Mary*,
Tony Abbott had finally managed to cram her quiver-
ing, squirming body into a closet. Now he slammed
the door on her, locked it, and leaned heavily against
it. Whew! He was sweating like a sandhog. God, he'd
give anything to take the damn rug off and mop his
scalp. Rivulets of perspiration were pouring out from
under the toupee and down his brow.

What the hell had happened? They'd left the bastard
in a stupor, about to sink without a trace into that
pretentious Roman bathtub. By everything that was
holy, he ought to have been dead half an hour ago. Now
here he was, bigger than life and twice as rotten,
dressed up in one of those ludicrous outfits of his
and granting an audience to that little hothead from
Muggleswump or wherever the hell she said she came
from.

And what exactly did Leo Farnsworth remember?
He *must* have been aware that he'd been drugged. He
must now remember that he'd been drugged and left
to die, and by whom. Shit! What were they going to do?
Here he was, poor innocent overworked Anthony Abbott, caught between the rock and the hard place, between a screaming, shrieking basket case like Julia
Farnsworth and the meanest man and dirtiest fighter in
the world, Leo Farnsworth. Inwardly, Abbott whimpered.

He had to go in there. As if nothing had happened. That was it. Keep cool. He had to pretend that nothing had happened, and give a damn convincing performance. Maybe Farnsworth would take it out on Julia. After all, what did he have against Abbott, right? Nothing except adultery and attempted murder.

He strode to the library door and knocked discreetly, then turned the knob. Farnsworth and Betty Logan were staring at him, waiting for his explanation of the screaming.

"Sorry to disturb you," Abbott said briskly. "Mrs. Farnsworth saw a mouse, but she's better now." It wasn't much, but it was the best he could do in such circumstances and with no notice.

"She saw a mouse?" echoed Betty. "Just now? Here?" She looked around a little apprehensively.

"No! Uh . . . not just . . . uh . . . before! Outside. But she relives it." Abbott realized that the more he talked the dumber he sounded. Collecting himself, he headed back to the living room. "I'll be in the other room if you need me, sir. Excuse me." He pulled the door shut behind him and made straight for the brandy. It would take more than one to pull him back into operating shape. Then he'd have to unlock the closet and let Julia out. That wasn't as easy as it sounded. God, he hated today!

"What's the matter with her?" Betty Logan faced Joe squarely.

Joe shrugged. "Well, it's really none of my business," he began.

"Your wife's none of your business?" demanded Betty indignantly. "Of course not. Any more than the lives of those hundreds of people whose lives you control, whose destinies you —"

"Look, she's not my wife," Joe interrupted.

"What!"

"I mean, she's not really my wife. She . . . you don't understand . . ." Joe finished feebly. He shot a helpless, pleading look at Mr. Jordan, who returned the look with one of sympathy. But no help.

"I understand one thing," snapped Betty. "We will never, *never* allow you to build that refinery. These people have only one home." Her eyes were bright with determination and anger.

"Well, all right," said Joe amiably. "I'll build my refinery in some other place. That's no big deal." He smiled, pleased with himself. After all, wasn't this exactly why he'd—temporarily—become Leo Farnsworth? To help Betty Logan out?

But Betty eyed him with suspicious dislike. She was not about to be toyed with. "Very funny, Mr. Farnsworth," she said, noticing the grin on his face. "If you think I'm going to turn around and go back to Pagglesham, you're wrong!"

"Good," said Joe sincerely. This was the best news he'd heard since he came out of that tunnel.

"I know you're not afraid of me," cried Betty, warmed by her indignation. "I know you think a schoolteacher from a small village is no challenge to a world-famous industrialist, but believe me, Mr. Farnsworth—"

"Hey, listen!" Joe attempted to cut through some of the verbiage. A schoolteacher? It figured. Boy, she sure knew how to deliver a lecture.

"By the time I get through . . ."

"Will you please listen?"

But there was no stopping her. " . . . with the eminent Leo Farnsworth . . ."

"Be quiet a minute, will you?" hollered Joe. Silence fell immediately as Betty stared at him open-mouthed. Joe took a deep breath and tried to talk quietly and rationally. "Just let me say one thing."

"What is it?" Betty was a little embarrassed at having been carried away by her rhetoric, but still huffy.

Joe took her elbow and led her toward the tufted Chesterfield sofa. "Sit down," he suggested.

"Why?" Suspicion was written all over her lovely features.

"If you'll just sit down a minute, I think I can tell you something that will clear this whole thing up." He waited until she had seated herself, and then he sat down next to her. Frowning, really not wanting to mess this up, he looked to Mr. Jordan for help, but none was forthcoming. He was on his own. "I'm not really Leo Farnsworth," he told her quickly, while he had the nerve. "My name is Joe."

Instantly, Betty Logan was on her feet, gathering up her coat and leather bag. Her face was tight with anger, a little muscle jumping at the corner of her jaw as she fought for self-control. "Mr. Farnsworth, I'm sure you enjoy playing these insulting little games, and I suppose the high point of your next meeting will be describing this one." She slammed the bag onto her shoulder and headed for the door to the hall. "But if you think you can treat women with the same manipulative contempt with which your company treats the citizens and communities of the world, you've got a lot to learn about the strength and persistence of people like myself. So don't think that you're going to get away with it. *Because you're not!*" She stormed out of the door, slamming it after her.

He *had* messed up. Of course. How could she imagine anything other than that he was playing games, dressed up in this stupid outfit, sitting in this gold-plated room surrounded by servants saying "Yes, Mr. Farnsworth" and "No, Mr. Farnsworth" and with a wife out there somewhere screaming her head off? This was a serious person, this Betty Logan. He'd messed up. Now she'd never believe him.

"What do I do now?" he asked Mr. Jordan plaintively.

"Whatever you think is right, Joe."

CHAPTER V

She was going to have a nervous breakdown, right here in the topiary maze. She *knew* it! Her nerves were too delicate, her constitution too frail to stand any more strain. Today was a monster. It must have added twenty years to her life. Her heart. Her heart was pounding so, she was going to have a heart attack this very minute. If that stupid idiot didn't take his hand off her mouth, she was going to have a heart attack, a nervous breakdown, suffocate, and die. Right here in the formal shrubbery, and then they'd be sorry. "Julia, darling," said Abbott, "I'm going to let you go now. Promise me you won't scream."

Scream? What was he talking about? Screaming? Who was screaming? She nodded, but his hand gripped her mouth more firmly.

"There's nothing to be frightened of, Julia," Tony went on. "There's plenty to be worried about, but nothing to be frightened of. Can I trust you?"

She nodded again, mffling against his smelly, sweaty palm. She hated his cologne. At last, Tony took his hand off her mouth.

"You locked me in a closet," Julia accused, her face crumpling.

"Only for a moment," he answered hastily.

"Why did you do that? What did you say to him?" she wailed.

Tony looked very uncomfortable, muttering so that she could barely make out what he was saying. "I . . . uh . . . told him you saw a mouse." At Julia's horrified expression, he added defensively, "I'm not very good at spur-of-the-moment alibis."

"Oh, my God!" moaned Julia. How on earth had she ever gotten mixed up with him? When had she been so desperate for affection that she'd taken on this fool?

"I'm very calm," said Tony stubbornly. "But I'm not very good," he confessed.

Julia looked at her lover in despair. "What's the difference?" she wailed. "He's probably got enough evidence against us to put us away for the rest of our lives. You locked me in a closet!" She began to snuffle again, remembering.

But Tony was gnawing on a knuckle, his eyes narrowed. "Darling, I don't understand this. I saw him inhale the nose spray. Two full squirts in each nostril."

"He never really inhaled it." Julia shook her head so violently that her hair tumbled into her face. "He overheard us somehow. He probably has everything bugged. We're probably being recorded right now." She looked around wildly. They were in a maze of high hedges, a copy in miniature of the giant maze at the palace at Hampton Court. It was the only place they could think of to find any privacy.

Great, thought Abbott. That's all he needed. Julia with electronic paranoia. On top of all her other neuroses. "Darling, we're not being recorded," he reassured her nervously, although he didn't believe a word of what he was saying. "An electronics expert sweeps the place every day. *He's* afraid of being bugged, too." At the mention of *him,* the pair turned their eyes guiltily toward one another, then away.

Julia would not be reassured. "He's playing with us," she insisted shrilly. "This is a game of some kind. He's playing a game. You locked me in a closet." She began to weep again.

"Mr. Abbott?"

Neither of them had seen the uniformed security guard come up behind them. They both jumped and

Julia opened her mouth to scream again, but Tony's reliable hand clamped down once more.

"Oh, hello," he said casually, as though he spent the better part of every day holding Mrs. Farnsworth's mouth shut.

"Mr. Farnsworth would like to see you now."

"Yes, indeed." Abbott grinned, showing all his teeth. "Will you excuse me, Mrs. Farnsworth?" he asked formally, removing his hand. She collected herself long enough to give him a regal nod of her head, but as she watched Tony follow the security guard back to the house, she bit off her thumbnail. Damn! Now she'd have to get it built up and wrapped, and it cost sixty dollars a nail. If she lived that long.

The polo hour over, Joe had changed to his croquet outfit, after several gentle hints from Sisk and some signs of real tears from Bentley. He was wearing a silk broadcloth, short-sleeved shirt with a microscopic monogram, tucked into English trousers of pongee, and wrapped around with a webbing belt. On his feet were rubber-soled shoes with tiny perforations by the hundreds. On his head was a Panama hat with a black silk band.

Joe handed Abbott a mallet, and the two of them went around the course. Joe's mind was still reeling; he was feeling punchy. Polo time, teatime, croquet . . . was Farnsworth an American industrialist or an English country squire? And Joe was constantly getting lost in that museum of a house. Countless rooms opened on endless corridors, and everywhere he went, new faces in servants' regalia kept calling him Mr. Farnsworth and expecting to be recognized. The quicker he was out of this body, the happier he'd be.

That was really the next item on the agenda. The Exo-Grey refinery business. He'd have to get that out of the way; the sooner the better so he could get Betty Logan what she wanted—liberation for Pagglesham. Then Mr. Jordan could find him a body that could beat Dallas—an unmarried body—and he could play football and get to know Betty Logan much better. Joe was sure she'd like him in any form but Farnsworth's.

So he'd sent for Abbott, who was now putting the yellow wooden ball through a series of wickets with malicious expertise, and watching him, Farnsworth, out of the corners of his terrified eyes. Joe knew why Abbott was sweating; he was sure that retribution was about to pour down on his head. But Joe had no time for revenge upon a pair of guilty lovers; that wasn't on his list of priorities. Besides, he wasn't Farnsworth. That thing Mr. Jordan had told him about Probability and Outcome stuck in the back of his head. Farnsworth had got his; they'd get theirs. It was only a matter of time. Still, Joe saw no reason to take Abbott or Julia off the hook. Let them sweat; they deserved it.

Joe measured the ground with the stick of his mallet, as he'd seen Abbott do, then gave the blue ball a sharp thwack. It went through, but just barely.

"Correct?" he asked.

"Legal," conceded Abbott.

"Yeah, but I mean, don't you think a person can do something that's legal and still be wrong?"

Abbott gasped suddenly for air, as though he'd been deflated by a pin. "Wrong in what sense, Mr. Farnsworth?" he breathed.

Joe hunted the blue ball through the next wicket. "You know . . . bad. Bad for somebody else."

He knows. Julia was right. He's playing with us. "I'm not sure what you're referring to, Mr. Farnsworth."

Joe was getting impatient with the slow pace of the game. He approached the ball with a gleam in his eye and gave it a good, hard hit, just like a golf ball, with body English and follow-through and the whole bit. "I mean like this Pagglesham thing where we're putting up that refinery." The ball left the gentle slope of the green and sailed through the air like a projectile. There was the sound of glass breaking.

"Is that the living-room window?" asked Joe cheerfully.

"I believe that was my office."

Joe shook his head. "Boy, is my coordination gone," he said sadly. This body was just not in shape.

"Yes, sir."

"Just not my day."

"I . . . uh . . . I wanted to discuss the Haitian arrangements," said Abbott, trying for firmer ground.

"The Haitian what?" This had taken Joe totally by surprise.

Tony's eyebrows went up. Maybe that drug had affected Farnsworth more than they suspected. He was certainly acting peculiar. This Haitian deal had been on the front burner of Farnsworth's mind for the past month. Now he was making noises as if he'd never heard of it. And the way he'd smacked that croquet ball . . . "The two and a half million acres," he supplied.

"What two and a half million acres?" asked Joe blankly.

"The sugar deal?" What was with him?

Joe shook his head. "It's no good," he said flatly.

"The deal?" Abbott's face expressed amazement.

"Sugar. It's no good for your body," said Joe.

"Did you want me to speak to the Haitian Ambassador?" asked Abbott delicately.

Joe shook his head again. "No. Find out if we're hurting anybody by putting up that refinery in Pagglesham," he ordered.

Now it was Abbott's turn to look blank. "Hurting anybody?" he repeated, uncomprehending.

"Yeah."

Tony was almost completely at a loss. Unless . . . yes, that must be it. He was still the same Farnsworth, Farnsworth the Fox. Julia must be right. The electronics boys had been here. Dropping to one knee, Tony ran a finger gingerly along the wicket. Then he looked up at Farnsworth. Forming the words clearly with his lips, he mouthed silently, "Are the wickets bugged?" They must be.

"Well, we certainly won't want to do that, sir." Abbott spoke loudly into the wicket. "The last thing Exo-Grey wants to do is hurt anybody. Isn't that right, sir?"

"That's right," agreed Joe. What an idiot!

It wasn't going to be as simple as he'd thought, being a giant of industry. It seemed that Leo Farnsworth was the head of a vast business complex, with something called interlocking directorships, which meant that Exo-Grey was actually made up of so many units that it was hard to tell who owned or ran what. Joe wished Gillette was here. Gillette was a tight end receiver who invested his money. He understood business, and many was the time he'd chewed Joe's ear off in the locker room. Gillette owned two laundromats and a fast-food franchise in Oklahoma City, a place that served soft ice cream, chili flavor, on a chocolate taco. Joe wished now that he'd paid more attention to Gillette's business talk in those days.

He wished old Snopes were here, too. Snopes came from South Carolina, from hill country, and played center for the Rams. He had fourteen brothers and sisters, all of whom married cousins, and Snopes could keep every one of his kinfolk straight in his head, including in-laws, for five generations back. Snopes could help him trace all these different companies down to their roots and unlock those directorships.

Meanwhile, Joe stayed in his room a lot, poring over computer printouts, company reports, messages to stockholders, and everything else that Sisk could provide that pertained to Exo-Grey. Actually, the room was kind of nice, now that Joe was getting used to it. It was done up all in brown, with leather on the walls, and pictures that Bentley called sporting prints hanging on the leather. The bed was large enough to accommodate Farnsworth's size, and Joe liked it, except for that damn mirror stuck to the ceiling. Now he sat in the middle of it, playing "Dinah" on the sax as he thumbed through pages of statistics and ran his eye down columns of figures. Not much of it made any sense to him, but he kept plugging away. Something . . . a glimmer . . . was beginning to penetrate. And there was always Abbott to answer his questions.

"Then he pretended for an hour not to know what a stockholder is!" Abbott whined to Julia. "I can't decide whether he's toying with me or if he actually would precipitate a crisis in the company."

Julia, dressed in a flowing silk caftan trimmed with real silver braid, fussed with the parrot tulips in the Lenox vase on top of the piano. "Of course he's toying with you," she snapped. "You don't think he's going to forget about being drugged, do you?"

"But why would he pretend like this?"

Julia tugged at the tassel on her heavy amber necklace in annoyance. "For the same reason he's pretending to bait us with the nose spray, waiting to see if we'll crack! Do you think he's actually *playing* that saxophone?" Both of them unconsciously looked up at the ceiling. From the room above came the faint, ghostly wailing of the sax, one wrong note after another. "There's a *tape* inside it. That's why we keep hearing the same song over and over! It's like his idiot costumes!" She glared at her lover in disgust. "You *are* dumb, aren't you?"

The boom of the cannon made them jump. That goddamn sunset gun! Ever since Farnsworth had read somewhere that the British raj fired off a cannon every night as they lowered the Union Jack, he'd had Sisk and Bentley take down the Stars and Stripes nightly with full ceremony, after which Sisk would come into the house and set out Pimms Cup No. 2, which always made Julia ill. God, she loathed Anglophilia!

Once the flag was lowered, it was time to dress for

dinner. Farnsworth would disappear into his suite to consult with Sisk and Bentley and would emerge two hours later, resplendent in what Julia privately referred to as "drag." About seven o'clock, she would send her own maid in to learn what sartorial glories Farnsworth would be dazzling them with this evening so that she herself might match his magnificence.

Tonight, the word was that it was rear admiral of the White, so Julia got out her biggest diamond necklace and paired it with her white Halston, the one-shoulder number. In the dress, she looked like last year's chorus girl in last year's creation, but to herself she was ravishing.

The formal dining room was Adam and Hepplewhite, but neither Julia nor Farnsworth was aware of it. Julia privately thought that the white mantel over the fireplace was too plain; one of these days she was going to have it sprayed gold. And the chairs were awfully old, even though they were in perfect condition. She hated the jacquard satin of the seats. Perhaps some chintz? Chintz was in these days; all the Beverly Hills decorators were combining it with wicker for that nonchalant look.

Leo Farnsworth had bought this house, furnishings and all, from the family who'd built it and who had furnished it with heirlooms from the mother country.

Actually, this house had not been Farnsworth's first choice. After he'd visited Chatsworth, one of the stateliest homes in England, he'd nearly caused a third war with Great Britain by offering to buy it, lock, stock and stables, and transport it stone by stone to southern California, like the *Queen Mary*. The House of Lords had risen as one man to demand this Yankee's head on a Wedgwood platter, and the National Trust had written an outraged letter to President Ford. A couple of Members of the House of Commons, Welshmen both, had suggested that Britain take the seventy million pounds that Farnsworth was offering, and spend it on making the coal mines safer for the miners. It took a great deal of diplomatic wiggling and dancing at the Court of St. James before the incident was closed.

Disappointed, Farnsworth had returned home to buy this seven-hundred-acre estate. It wasn't the tennis courts or the swimming pool or the stables or the greenhouses that had attracted him to the place, it was the cricket pitch and the croquet lawn. He didn't know that the portraits were by Reynolds, but he did know that they were of English gentlemen and ladies. He loved the fact that the servants' quarters were belowstairs, and that a butler and valet came with the house. He was fond of the faded brocades at the windows and was angered when Julia had thrown them out, claiming that two hundred years was long enough for a fabric.

Most important, when he stood for the first time in the center of the house, under the chandelier in the entrance foyer, Farnsworth had felt a great sadness stealing over him, and he wept that the British had lost India. That was when he'd known that this place must be his, down to the last bronze doorknob.

The place had been on the market for two years at an asking price of thirty-five million, but for Farnsworth the price went to sixty, since new money has so much less value than old. And he had paid it gladly.

Of course, Farnsworth had wanted to add a few personal touches to make the estate truly his. The moose head in the library was a happy addition, hanging over the matched Purdey pistols as was the valet stand in his bedroom. He always wondered why Bentley never used it; why, in fact, the man shuddered every time he passed it. He also owned a fine collection of wooden decoy ducks, and he thought they added something to the living room, a welcome hominess. When he had more time to watch television, he would be putting in an Advent room-size screen.

But the dining room intimidated him, with its Romneys and its Reynolds on the walls, and the long

Hepplewhite sideboard's gleaming polished surface under the weight of the silver-covered dishes. What Farnsworth had brought to the dining room was himself in all his splendor, night after night, to sit at the table set for forty, set for three. He sat at the head, of course, and Julia at the foot, and Abbott somewhere down the long side in the middle, and they'd shout at each other to make conversation. Night after night.

How could he take it, night after night? Joe wondered as he peered down the long mahogany table. Why had Sisk and Bentley stuffed him into this sailor suit? He was wearing a white admiral's uniform, dress, with a red sash that ran diagonally across his chest and carried a series of unearned decorations. The collar was stiff and cut into his neck, and he couldn't eat the food. There were cutlets of some kind, fried, and Joe never touched anything fried. He managed with two large bowls of salad, and no more than a couple of mouthfuls of puréed carrots. Tomorrow he'd lay in a supply of soybeans to munch on, and sunflower seeds. And some tofu.

But food wasn't uppermost in Joe's mind, finance was.

"What you're saying is that nobody is supposed to know about it, because if two big companies get together, they're worth a lot more money." Joe had been reading up on mergers.

How long was Farnsworth planning to keep up this charade of ignorance? Well, Tony Abbott would just have to go along with it until . . . if at first you don't succeed, Julia kept saying. She was on the thin edge now. Farnsworth was paying her no attention at all; he barely ever spoke to her, and when he did, it was with such cheerful affability that Julia's paranoia had increased to the point of near madness. Like Lady Macbeth, she was talking of blood, Farnsworth's blood. But Tony was keeping cool. It was the one role he knew how to play.

"Yes, sir," he answered Joe now. "That's why the rumor of a merger makes the price of a stock rise."

"If it's supposed to be a secret, how does the rumor start?" asked Joe, his brow furrowed by the paradox.

"Well, sir, wrong as it seems . . . they leak it."

"That's dishonest!" exclaimed Joe.

"Yes, sir," agreed Abbott piously.

Joe put down his dessert spoon. He'd eaten it all, but fruit compote was on the okay list. He gathered up the scattered papers under his elbow into one neat pile. "Well, if I've got a board meeting tomorrow, I'd better do some studying," he said.

Tucking his plumed admiral's hat under one arm, Joe stood up. He caught a glimpse of Julia's face down at the other end of the long stretch of table. She was looking kind of pale. "How ya doing down there?" he called out in a friendly voice. It was the first sentence he'd addressed to her all evening.

Julia felt the spoon slipping from her nerveless fingers to crash on the Spode plate. "Fine," she croaked. He hadn't touched his wine, she noticed. Four glasses, one filled for each course, still brimmed at his place. What was he planning that he needed a clear head?

"Thanks for the dinner," Joe yelled in the direction of the pantry. He was always thanking the servants these days; it was driving them crazy.

As he left the dining room, Julia leaned forward over the table. In the light of the candles, her eyes glittered, desperate, mad eyes. "I think we should do it very soon," she hissed at Abbott. "Right away!"

CHAPTER VI

A mixture of anxiety and anticipation churned in Joe's guts on Friday morning, the day of the board meeting. He'd worked hard to digest this Exo-Grey stuff, but he had no idea how much of the data would stick in his mind, or what a corporate board meeting was like. That caused the anxiety. On the other hand, Joe loved nothing better than a good scrimmage, and life wasn't so different from football, was it? Not if you followed rules. And he had an idea that he might be seeing Betty Logan again today, and that added to the anticipation. Although he'd been up all night reading, he felt exhilarated after his shower. He watched Sisk and Bentley pick out a dark blue double-breasted pinstripe and regimental tie, a wide grin on his face. He looked pretty good in these fancy threads of Farnsworth's. Even if he did say so himself. And he wanted to look good for Betty.

Abbott was waiting for him downstairs, clutching a leather portfolio of documents. Joe followed him out to the helipad on the front lawn, where his private Sikorsky was waiting, its rotors turning. Sisk and Bentley were on hand to add the finishing touch. Sisk was clutching a homburg and a helmet, which he passed over to Joe. Then they ducked out of the downdraft.

Strapping on the helmet, Joe climbed into the front seat next to the pilot while Abbott crammed himself into the back of the copter. As they took off, Joe felt a rush of pleasure. He loved to fly, but had been in a helicopter only three times in his life before. Like a kid, he watched Los Angeles spreading out under them as they flew over the city and landed on the roof of the Exo-Grey Building. He felt ready for damn near anything.

A private elevator took Abbott and Joe down from the roof to the lower floors, and an impressive cantilevered staircase brought them down to conference-room level. There was a crowd waiting at the foot of the steps, and Joe searched it eagerly for Betty, but he didn't see her. Popping flashbulbs and a minicam told Joe that the crowd was made up of newspaper and TV reporters.

"Hello, Mr. Farnsworth." A tall brunette had separated herself from the crowd and was waving a paper under Joe's nose. "I'm Helen Rich from the *Times*. We have this petition from the citizens of Pagglesham. Are you planning to do anything about this?"

"Yeah. Hey, where did you get that?" he asked the reporter, looking around for Betty again.

"We're taking that under consideration." Abbott's response was given at the top of his lungs, to drown out Joe's.

"Is it true," asked another reporter, "that the three newly proposed Exo-Grey factories will displace eleven communities?"

Joe stopped in his tracks and turned to face the newsman. "Eleven? I didn't know it was that many."

"Well, they granted you the permits to build, didn't they?" pressed the reporter.

"I guess so. If we got them."

"How do you suppose Exo-Grey got those permits, Mr. Farnsworth?" A microphone was being shoved in Joe's face now.

Joe shrugged his shoulders. "Beats me. I guess we bribed somebody," he said simply.

A horrified gasp rose collectively from the reporters and was echoed briefly by the look on Abbott's face. Then Tony's cool returned.

"Very funny," he chuckled. "Mr. Farnsworth's joking, of course. Let us by, please. We really must be getting to the meeting."

Taking Joe firmly by the arm, Tony led him through the pack of reporters, only to be blocked by another group of newshounds, this one formed around Betty Logan. Before Joe could call out or wave to her, the girl confronted him squarely, her blue eyes blazing with righteousness.

"What about acrylonitrile, Mr. Farnsworth?" she demanded.

This stopped Joe like a two-hundred-and-seventy-pound tackle. "What about *what*?"

"Acrylonitrile. The toxic substance released by the new plastic soda bottles your company is marketing despite the Consumer Protection League's lawsuit to force you to delay distribution until the effects on the human body have been tested."

You had to hand it to her. This girl really did her homework. Joe's admiration for her zoomed even higher than before.

"We really must be going," snapped Tony.

But Joe had raised his voice now so that everybody could hear him. "Look, I've been making a study of this thing for a couple of days, and I think I got it pretty well figured out. Why don't all of you come inside and hear for yourselves just what's going on?"

I'm going crazy, thought Abbott. I didn't hear that. I didn't hear Leo Farnsworth inviting the media into a closed board meeting of Exo-Grey. "We'd better get inside, Mr. Farnsworth," he said hastily, pushing Joe ahead of him, away from the press. "The board is waiting."

The board was indeed waiting, but not for the crowd that suddenly burst in on them. Who were all these people, dragging in heavy cables and shoulder cameras, lights and microphones, pencils and note pads? Why were they lining up against the wall to get a better view of the large slate conference table and the twenty board members seated around it in Charles Eames chairs? There were never any spectators at an Exo-Grey board meeting, let alone members of the press! What the hell was going on here? Thank God, there was Leo Farnsworth at last. He'd pull this meeting together. Nobody loathed the press with the passion of Leo Farnsworth. After all, of all of them, he had the most to hide.

"Hi, everybody," yelled Joe. "How ya doing? A lot of these people are reporters from the newspapers and TV, and I invited them in to see how we do things."

What? What was he saying? Had Farnsworth taken leave of his senses?

"Leo, this is a very, very dangerous precedent," whispered the board member closest to Joe.

But it was too late. Reporters were already beginning to fire their questions.

"Mr. Farnsworth, isn't it true that an accident in your West Coast nuclear plant might stimulate seismic activity in the San Andreas fault which could destroy most of southern California?"

No kidding! Joe had never heard that. Just as he opened his mouth to ask for more information, Tony Abbott cut in quickly.

"I think you have to define 'destroy,' " he said curtly.

Now a portly, white-haired gentleman in a glen plaid suit was rapping for attention on the conference table. This was Henry Oppenheim, president of the board of Exo-Grey, second in command to Farnsworth, who was chairman.

"Excuse me, ladies and gentlemen," said Oppenheim smoothly. "If we're going to get into this subject right away, let me just say this. I'd like to make it perfectly clear that the Exo-Grey nuclear facility has a foolproof built-in safety system that guarantees no danger of any kind."

Joe took a step forward. "No danger? What do you mean?" he asked Oppenheim directly. "If there's no danger, how come we're in the middle of a lawsuit?"

"We're not," snapped Oppenheim hotly. "It's a protest, not a lawsuit." What the hell did Leo think he was doing? What kind of slick power play was this?

"That's not the point," said Joe stubbornly. "The point is, we're doing something wrong. Everybody is suing us. I mean, here, for instance, everywhere you look . . ." He pointed to the papers scattered on the massive black slate table. "The refinery, the nuclear plant . . . look right here." Joe picked up a folder and waved it at the board. "Here's a guy named Porpoise who's suing us—"

"Mr. Farnsworth," interrupted Charles Montgomery, head of the legal division of the company. "That's an ecological suit against our canning company for destroying porpoises."

Joe sank down into his chair, looking dazed. "We can porpoises?" he said in a choked voice. He loved porpoises. He often went down to Marineland to visit them. They were almost human.

Across the table, Oppenheim caught Tony Abbott's eye and gave him a signal. He stood up and left the room; less than a minute later, Abbott joined them outside.

"What is it, Henry?" he asked suavely, as though nothing were wrong.

"Will you tell me what's going on?" demanded Oppenheim, red-faced with rage. "What the hell is he doing bringing the press in here?"

Tony shrugged. "Henry, you know Leo Farnsworth."

"Obviously I *don't* know Leo Farnsworth," snapped the other.

Neither do I, any more, thought Abbott. But how can I admit that to anybody? I'm supposed to be his right hand, and I don't know what the left one is doing.

Inside the board room, Weston Renfield, senior vice-president, was explaining, "As everybody knows, we can tuna. And, in netting tuna, we're forced to kill . . . a number . . . of porpoises. And, since they're mammals of allegedly high intelligence, there's been an outcry. But we do have a corporate responsibility which extends to thousands of shareholders of moderate means. People who, in many instances, are not nearly as well off as the ecological groups which are opposing us."

"Absolute rubbish!" Betty Logan was on her feet now, warming to the fight. "You talk about your concern for the environment, when your evident concern is for your excessive profits. You—"

"Well, look," interrupted Joe, standing up. He'd just come up with something, and he wanted to try it out on everybody. "It's like when we were supposed to stop eating grapes. Well, some guys did, but I didn't because I didn't know anything about it and I like grapes. Well, a lot of guys like tuna, and they're going to go on eating it, anyway. But . . . what if there was a good-guy tuna company that was on the porpoise team? Some of these guys would buy that so their kids wouldn't get mad at them. Right?"

"Ridiculous!" snorted Montgomery.

"Well, wait a minute," said Renfield slowly, leaning over the table. "That's not a bad name, Good-Guy Tuna."

Now Hedley Lawson, treasurer of Exo-Grey, spoke up for the first time. "Gentlemen, I don't think we're taking into account the expense of catching tuna without killing porpoises."

"Yeah," said Joe, "but we don't care how much it costs, do we? We just care how much it makes."

Flashbulbs began to go off, and the minicams zoomed in on Joe. Reporters were scribbling furiously into their notebooks.

"And if it costs too much," Joe went on, "charge a penny more. Make it part of the game plan. Would you pay a penny to save a fish who thinks?" Now he was getting warmer, his face lighting up with enthusiasm. "And we could do the same thing with all the lawsuits. Let the other team build the power plant in all the wrong places. Let the other quarterback throw a girl out so it gets in the press and the stock-holders don't like it." Joe's eyes found Betty's across the table; she was staring at him quizzically, uncertainly. "Let us be the team that plays fair!" Joe thundered, smacking the table with his open palm. "The guys who get the contract. The popular players." He straightened up, triumphant.

"Leo, Leo." Lawson was shaking his head. "Exo-Grey is not a football team."

Joe sat back down again, blocked for the moment. That was true. Unless . . . "Well, look, lemme ask you this. If we *were* a football team, would you say that we have a winning season so far?"

"Are you serious?" Lawson demanded.

Joe nodded. "Go ahead. Just generally, would you say we have a winning season?"

"Well, all right, yes." Lawson was uncomfortable with the football metaphor. "We are having an extremely good year."

Joe stood up again, hunching over the table like a quarterback in a huddle. His eyes drilled into the faces of the board members as though they were his team players. "Then, what do you do?" he demanded. "What do you do when you're ahead in the game?"

"Leo . . . " protested Lawson.

"What do you do?" Joe turned directly to Lawson. "Well . . . I don't know . . . what you're . . . driving at. . . ."

Now Joe addressed everybody in the room, while the cameras went on clicking. "You know what you do? You don't make mistakes. You don't gamble unnecessarily. You don't pass deep in your own territory. You protect your lead. You protect your players. You make sure nobody gets hurt. You're going to need them in the next game. We won this one. That's the responsible thing to do. We're gonna forget about that nuclear plant until it's safe. We're gonna relocate that Pagglesham refinery, fellas, put it somewhere else. It's gonna cost us thirty-five million, but it doesn't matter. And we're gonna stop making containers out of that plastic gunk until we know what it is. We're not playing just one game. Let's go all the way, fellas. Let's get to the Super Bowl, and when we get there, let's already have won." Joe picked up his homburg and his helmet. "Okay, I gotta go. I gotta see somebody."

He strode out of the room, with Abbott scrambling after him. In his ears, inaudible to anybody else, was the cheering of a hundred thousand fans. Cheering for the Good Guys.

Behind him, bedlam reigned.

"What happened?" Julia demanded when Tony came into the house, his face ashen. "How did it go?"

Tony stood shaking his head very slowly from side to side.

"What *happened?*" She grabbed his arm in a tight squeeze and dug in her long red fingernails.

"If he wasn't going to be dead soon, he'd need years of psychiatric help."

"If he isn't going to be dead soon, *I'll* need years of psychiatric help," Julia swore. "Let's do it!" she pleaded. "Let's kill him tonight!"

"Mr. Pendleton," said the Escort.

Joe looked up from the sports news on TV. The Escort and Mr. Jordan were standing one on either side of the set. Joe grinned happily.

"Hey, am I glad to see you!"

"We have good news for you." Mr. Jordan smiled.

Joe jumped up, excited. "Yeah? Great! I got to find a real good body right away!"

As if on cue, Lavinia, the maid, tiptoed into the room, smiling invitingly. At once, Joe realized that every word he would be saying could now be heard. But where can you find privacy in a house that has a wife, a private secretary, and a staff of seventeen, not counting the gardeners? Wait, he had it!

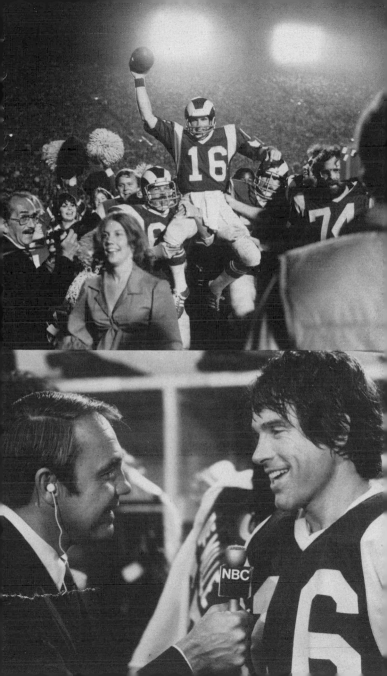

Leaving the puzzled and chagrined Lavinia behind, Joe led Mr. Jordan and the Escort out of the master suite and down the long landing to a mop closet at the far end. He opened the door and peered inside. Except for the brooms and the buckets, it was empty. The three of them slipped inside, and Joe closed the door carefully behind him.

"Look," he began, "I kept my word to Betty Logan. Like I promised. Now you really gotta find me a body that's in good shape."

"We have a number of interesting possibilities coming up now, Joe," said Mr. Jordan.

"I gotta have somebody with good legs. How long do you think it will take?"

"I'm certain it won't take long, Mr. Pendleton," said the Escort reassuringly. "We're doing the best we can. It's hard to say exactly, but we have three probabilities now. That's why we're here."

"Things will work out, Joe," Mr. Jordan promised.

Joe nodded. "Yeah, I'm sure of that. I trust you. But I gotta get a body fast, or I'm not going to make it to the Super Bowl."

There was a knock on the mop closet door.

"Who's that?" Joe called out, suddenly nervous.

"It's Sisk, sir."

Do butlers have radar? "Come in, Sisk."

The door to the closet opened, and Sisk entered with the air of one coming into the most elegant drawing room. Nothing fazed him. Millionaires were expected to be eccentric, and Sisk enjoyed having his expectations fulfilled.

"Sorry to disturb you, Mr. Farnsworth," he said smoothly, as if he found his employer talking to nobody in a mop closet every day of the week, "but Miss Betty Logan is downstairs, sir, and asks if you might spare her a moment of your time."

Betty Logan! Joe suddenly reordered his priorities. "Uh, sure. Tell her I'll be right down."

"Very good, sir. Do you wish the door closed?"

"Closed is fine, thank you." He turned again to Mr. Jordan. "Look. Do the best you can. I gotta go down and see what she wants."

Things were working out, he told himself as he ran down the stairs. He was going to be released from this body, and find a better one, and make it to the Super Bowl, and win for the Rams, and get to know Betty.

CHAPTER VII

All the way out to the Farnsworth estate, Betty Logan had nervously rehearsed what she was going to say to him. When his eyes had looked for hers in the conference room, she felt a strange electricity pass between them. She had felt it once before, when they first met, but she'd dismissed the feeling and replaced it with anger at what he was.

But what was he? What sort of man was Leo Farnsworth? Different from anybody she had ever met, quixotic, puzzling, and yes, eccentric. He was magnetic, she couldn't deny that, not even to herself, but Betty had fought his magnetism. He was a millionaire, totally opposed to everything she believed in, and married as well.

Yet hadn't he proved today that his opinions and hers were not so strongly in opposition after all? And what was it he had said to her that first time they'd met? "She's not my wife." What had he meant by that?

But she didn't expect to see him after today, did she? Her work was finished here, and she had come only to thank him and to say goodbye. Why, then, were her hands so cold? And why could she feel the pulse at the base of her throat beating like a drum?

He walked into the room, tall, commanding, with those incredibly clear blue eyes that looked right through you. Betty jumped to her feet and started talking before she lost her nerve.

"Mr. Farnsworth, I don't know what you must think of me after my behavior on our first meeting, but before I leave for England I feel I must tell you what an incredibly extraordinary thing it is you did today."

Joe's eyes had never been trained to notice women's clothes but she was wearing something so soft and so simple that it brought out the colors of her eyes and hair. Blue and gold. Hey, those were the colors of the Rams' uniforms, blue and gold. It was a sign! She was talking so fast he couldn't make out what she was saying, but . . . was she telling him she was going back to England? And saying thanks?

"You don't have to thank me," he said hastily. "It's okay, you know? Look, you seem to be a little pale. Sort of pale. You want something to eat?"

Something to eat? Betty realized suddenly that she was ravenous. She nodded her head.

"Great! I'll be right back." Joe sprinted out of the living room and down the hallway to the dining room, shouting for the servants.

"Bentley! Everett!"

They appeared like magic; they always did. Joe sometimes wondered if servants ever slept. "Miss Logan is going to eat with us," he informed them. "Put on another plate. And Bentley . . . whip up a liver and whey shake."

"Yes, Mr. Farnsworth."

When Joe got back to the living room, Betty was standing with her coat on and her purse tucked under her arm.

"Where are you going?" he asked her in alarm.

Puzzled, Betty tried to explain. "Well, I thought you said . . ." She trailed off, embarrassed.

Now Joe caught on. "Oh. You thought I meant we were going out to eat, huh?"

"Well, yes . . ."

"Sure. Okay. Fine with me. Right. That's a good idea." He shepherded her out of the living room and into the magnificent foyer. "Sisk! We're gonna go out! Bentley! Everett! We're gonna go out and eat." He tugged at Betty's elbow, hurrying her along.

Almost as eerily as Mr. Jordan did, Sisk materialized seemingly from nowhere, clutching a selection of hats in his hands. There was a straw boater, a fedora, a topee, a deerstalker, and a tam. "Which hat would you prefer, sir?" he asked silkily.

Automatically, Joe reached for the tam and the boater. Then he thrust them back at the butler. "I don't want to wear a hat," he growled. "I never want to wear a hat again. I'm sick of hats. Listen, Sisk, don't show me any more hats. Understand?"

"Yes, sir. No more hats." The butler's eyes widened in surprise. Up to now, nothing had ruffled his composure, not even the voice coming out of the mop closet. But . . . no *hats?* What was the world coming to?

Joe was not even aware that he was eating junk food as he sat next to Betty in the back seat of the Daimler. Both of them bit deeply into their hamburgers, which were smothered in onions, pickles, lettuce, and a horrible dressing made, apparently, of white shoe polish. Joe thought it was delicious.

"Do you eat here often?" Betty smiled. She found the paradox delightful, the Georgian tea service and the greasy hamburger. This man was full of surprises.

Joe lowered his voice so that his chauffeur wouldn't hear him. "I just—just didn't think you'd want people to see you out with a guy like me," he told her. He leaned forward and touched the driver on the shoulder. "Hey, get us some malts, will ya please?" Obediently, the chauffeur got out and joined the line at the hamburger stand. He looked so out of place in his gold-buttoned tunic and polished puttees that Betty couldn't help herself; she laughed out loud.

This was the first time that they'd ever been alone together, really alone. They sat without speaking, but Joe couldn't take his eyes off Betty.

"I'm sorry," he said at last. "I can't seem to stop staring at you."

"Well," Betty replied softly, "I appear to be staring, too."

The most incredible feeling came over Joe Pendleton; he was choked by so much emotion that he couldn't speak. It was as if this girl were the center of the universe, the focus of all his dreams and plans. It was as if his entire life had come to the tiny pinpoint of now. And this wasn't even *him,* he thought suddenly. She wasn't even seeing *him.* She was seeing Leo Farnsworth. He had the sudden desire to take her up to Topanga Canyon and show her his little house, his *own* little house. He guessed the feeling was love.

"What are you thinking?" asked Betty.

Joe struggled to find the right words. "Oh . . . just . . . this isn't what I thought was gonna happen to me." It didn't sound very romantic, but it was the best he could do.

It seemed to be enough for Betty. "I know. I think I stopped believing something like this could happen to me."

"You mean . . . you mean . . . it's happening to you, too?"

"I'm afraid so," whispered Betty. Her eyelashes touched her cheeks.

"And with me . . . of all people?" Joe asked quietly. She would never know how bitter that question was, or who it was that was asking it. Was he Pendleton or Farnsworth? Which man did she love, this beautiful, precious, desirable girl?

Betty nodded and smiled. "You know, even when I was really trying to hate you, I couldn't help seeing something else . . . something . . ."

"What?" Joe asked eagerly. So much, so very much depended on her answer.

"Something in your eyes. Does that sound silly?"

Joe sank back into the deep upholstery of the limo. "No," he said. "No, that doesn't sound silly." The eyes, she said. The eyes are the windows of the soul. His mother always used to say that. She was right. Betty had seen his soul, locked in Farnsworth's body, maybe, but Joe Pendleton's own soul. It was the soul, not the body, she'd fallen in love with. Joe, not Farnsworth. That was all he needed to know. Now he knew what he had to do, and it wouldn't be easy.

"Here you are, sir." The chauffeur had appeared with two paper bags and was handing them into the car.

Joe took the bags and tossed them aside. Abruptly, he turned to Betty. "Hey, look, I gotta talk to somebody right away. Would you mind if I took you home?"

A small shadow of hurt crossed Betty's eyes, but she shook her head and said "All right" in a small voice.

On the ride back to Betty's motel, Joe seemed distracted, lost in thought. When she got out of the car, he escorted her to the door but made no move to kiss her. It was obvious to Betty that his thoughts were somewhere else. She reminded herself of his eccentricities, his strange pattern of behavior, but she couldn't shake off the hurt of his apparent rejection.

"Good night," said Joe matter-of-factly.

"Good night," said Betty. "And thank you."

"Don't mention it." He turned to go, but stopped as if on an impulse and delivered himself of an afterthought. "Oh, by the way, I'm getting a divorce."

Joe's words stopped Betty cold. "But you and your wife aren't even separated," she gasped.

"Oh, sure we are. It's a big house."

Betty watched him get into the back seat of the limo and be driven off in luxury. He was incredible! The most unpredictable . . . insane . . . Suddenly she laughed. The feeling of rejection had totally vanished.

"Mr. Pendleton, we've gone to some trouble to find you an athlete," said the Escort reproachfully.

"I know. I'm sorry. I know what I said. But that was before. Look, couldn't you hold up on that for a little while? Something happened tonight and I've changed my mind." Joe shifted a broom so that he could stand a little more comfortably. Thirty-eight rooms in this house, and he had to hole up in a mop closet! "I'm gonna have to stay Farnsworth for a little while longer, and I'm gonna have to get Farnsworth into shape. And I can do it." A sudden thought took hold of him. "And I'm gonna get Max Corkle to help me, to train me."

"He's back in the mop closet again, huh?" Corinne asked Bentley.

"Yes."

Bentley climbed the stairs and found Everett waiting patiently outside the master bedroom suite, holding a tray with a pot of cocoa and two cups. "He's not there. He's back in the mop closet."

"But what will I do with his cocoa?" fretted Everett. "I don't like to disturb him, but dare I let his cocoa get cold?"

"I notice there are two cups?"

"Well, Sisk felt that since Mr. Farnsworth was pretending to talk to somebody, he might want to pretend to offer him cocoa, too."

Joe came out of the mop closet in a marvelous mood, exhilarated and ebullient. As a man of action, he'd been stagnating lately, going to pot. Now all that was going to change. He had a game plan, a real game plan, and he was going to be in control, call the plays like a quarterback oughta.

He zipped past Bentley and Everett and the carob cocoa with a cheery wave and dashed down the hall to Julia's room. He was about to turn the knob when a thought struck him. Better knock. It's only polite.

At the sound of the knock, Tony Abbott leaped out of Julia's bed and ran behind the window drape.

"Yes, just a minute," called Julia frantically, patting the other pillow smooth and pulling her nightgown straps up over her voluptuous shoulders.

Joe grinned down at her. "Hi. Look, I'm sorry to

bother you so late. But I don't love you and you don't love me, so let's get a divorce. All right?"

"I don't know what you're talking about, Leo," gasped Julia, aghast.

"Yes, you do," Joe assured her, turning to go. Then, remembering something, he turned back and called to the drapery: "Oh, Abbott, there's a trainer for the Rams named Max Corkle. Call him tomorrow and ask him to come over here and see me. Okay?"

"Yes, Mr. Farnsworth," answered the drapery obediently.

"Thanks. Good night." And he was out the door, humming.

"You *idiot!* Why in God's name did you answer!?!" shrieked Julia.

Tony came out from behind the curtain sheepishly. "I couldn't help it. His will is too strong," he confessed. His rug had slipped and was dangling over one ear. Julia shut her eyes and begged for strength. "Thank God we didn't wait," she crowed. "In a few minutes we'll be rid of him. He'll be dead . . ." She began to cackle insanely, and Abbott leaped across the room to put his hand over her mouth.

"Julia!" he cautioned. "There might be . . ." He mouthed the word "microphones."

Julia pulled his hand away from her mouth in disgust. "Don't be insane. This room is examined every day. I tell you there are no microphones," she snarled.

Abbott looked around the room. How could she tell? Julia's bedroom was a garden of tulips. The sheets and pillowcases were tulip-printed to match the coverlet and the wallpaper. The chaise longue and its cushions were upholstered in tulips, as was the headboard of the queen-size bed. There were tulip-patterned pillows everywhere. All you'd have to do would be to hide a bug in a real tulip, and nobody would ever find it, ever. Sometimes, when Tony was making love to Julia, he felt like a drone cuddling up to a queen bee, lost in a bed of tulips. "Dearest, let's not quarrel now," he

91

pleaded. "It's almost over. Did you look under the bed?"

Dropping to his knees, Abbott began to search the tulip-patterned carpet for a hidden microphone. Julia stuffed a corner of the tulip sheet into her mouth and bit down hard.

Joe's energy level was so high now that he felt like going out and running around the estate, even if it was past one in the morning. Maybe he'd strip down and start running tonight. No time like the present to start getting in shape. There wasn't much time left before the Big Game. Right. That was what he'd do. If necessary, he'd take a flashlight.

He strode into his room and took off his topcoat. For one moment he thought of calling his valet to help him undress, but that was all over now. From now on, Farnsworth would take care of himself, or rather, Joe would take care of Farnsworth. No more heavy meals. No more riding around in limos. No more being waited on hand and foot. Gleefully, he tossed his coat on the bed. It landed heavily. An instant later, the heavy mirror on the ceiling over the bed came crashing down, flattening the bed like a pancake. The din was tremendous. If Joe had been on that bed . . .

Of course. The coat. The bed had been booby-trapped. Joe was *supposed* to have been on the bed when the mirror came hurtling down. Leo Farnsworth was supposed to have been snuffed. Instead, the coat had been snuffed. Oh, for God's sake, was he going to have more trouble with those two dimwits? Didn't he have enough trouble trying to pull this out-of-shape body into peak condition in only a handful of time?

Back in Julia's bedroom, the dimwits were covering each other with guilty kisses and bites, and Julia was moaning into Abbott's ear. "We couldn't help it, could we, Tony? We were right to—"

A knock at the door. With the agility of practice, Tony leaped behind the tulip-printed draperies, and Julia, pretending to be aroused from innocent sleep, called, "Yes, Sisk?"

Joe walked in and talked to the drapery. "Abbott, Corkle's number is 654-1654."

"Yes, Mr. Farnsworth," said the drapery.

As the door closed behind the immortal, unkillable, omnipotent, omniscient, omnipresent Leo Farnsworth, Julia began to scream and scream and scream.

Max Corkle let out a startled whistle as he drove his little LTD up the driveway of the Farnsworth estate. He'd heard about this place, but he'd never expected to see it in his lifetime. There were seven hundred acres of prime real estate here, and the mansion that revealed itself at the bend of the driveway looked more like a museum than a mere house.

What the hell could Farnsworth want with him? At first, he was sure that the telephone call had been a gag. The guys on the team were always pulling crap like that; they thought it was funny. But the guy on the other end had sounded so snotty and insistent that Corkle had decide to take a chance. Then, when he'd passed the security check at the main gate, when he'd seen his own name and license plate number on the checklist, he'd begun to wonder. A guy like Leo Farnsworth, and a guy like Max Corkle—it didn't figure.

There was a pair of armed guards stationed at the front door, but they'd been briefed on the walkie-talkie, so they were polite. A real live butler came to the door, just like Jeeves in the movies. He wore a kind of soup-and-fish, almost a tuxedo, but with tails. Corkle wondered how the job paid.

"Follow me," said the butler. "Right this way, sir."

Awed into silence, Max followed the soup-and-fish down through the marble-floored hallway, past tall vases of fresh flowers, long Oriental runners so precious that they had faded hundreds of years before, and polished mirrors with heavy gilt frames.

"Mr. Farnsworth is waiting for you in the ballroom," announced Sisk.

The ballroom! If that don't take the pink plastic bagel, thought Corkle. What did he bring me here for, to teach me the cha-cha-cha? He gave the Rams cap a defiant twitch to one side and smoothed down the front of his team jacket.

The ballroom was so vast that Corkle could field the Rams here for practice. The ceiling was more than twenty feet high and garlanded in stucco. The entire vaulted roof was covered in paintings depicting the love life of Zeus with various goddesses and ladies, all dressed in wisps of netting, all of them at least a D cup. The width of the room was forty feet, the length sixty. From the paintings on the ceiling hung a row of ornate crystal chandeliers, each set about ten feet away from the next. The walls were divided into panels above the wainscoting. Every second panel was antique silk, and in between the fabric panels were painted panels that corresponded to the ceiling. Only here the ladies had a bit less to cover and a bit less covering it. Also, a few of them were seen from the rear, which was Max's favorite part of the chicken. He couldn't imagine the kind of person who would design a room like this one, or the kind of parties that had been thrown in it.

There was a very different kind of party being held here now. At one glance, Corkle could tell that the ballroom was being turned into a professional gym. All along the width of the room, men on ladders were spanning it with heavy beams, and covering the beams with "L" brackets. Powerful drills lay on the floor, attached to thick electric cables, and Corkle could see where the bolts would be put that would hold the rings and ropes. Two guys were uncrating a Nautilus Super Pullover Machine, and an electric rowing machine was plugged in and ready to go. A set of Nissen parallel bars and a horse stood over to the side, with mats tumbled around it. A leg-extension machine was still in its packing crate. Corkle shook his head in amazement. There must be forty or fifty thousand dollars' worth of professional gym equipment here, at least. And who knows what else was going to be delivered?

At the far side of the room was the most beautiful weight rack that Max had ever seen. It stood six feet high and was made of solid oak. Arranged in pairs inside it were dumbbells of plated silver, ranging in size from five to sixty-five pounds, as bright and shiny as a Christmas tree. Standing in front of the rack, checking out the bells, was a tall man in his thirties, dressed in a Gucci custom-made exercise suit, with a Chinese silk bathrobe over it. Max guessed that this was Farnsworth.

"Mr. Corkle, sir," announced the butler, and the tall man turned.

When he heard Sisk announce Corkle, Joe turned around and grinned. To his surprise, he felt a sudden prickle behind his eyes at the sight of the stocky, gruff guy in the Rams jacket. He swallowed the lump in his throat and called out, "Max! How ya doing?"

"Fine, thanks," replied Corkle politely.

Joe started across the ballroom, his long legs a rapid blur. Grabbing Corkle's hand, he shook it warmly. "Hey, you lost a little weight?" he commented.

Corkle was taken aback. "Have we met?" he asked tentatively.

"Sort of," replied Joe. "Sort of. Thank you, Sisk."

Throwing his arm around Corkle's shoulder affectionately, Joe led him across the room to look at the universal gym, a complicated and expensive arrangement of weights and pulleys. "I hear you got all of Joe Pendleton's athletic equipment," he said.

"Yeah," said Corkle suspiciously. "How'd you know that?"

"I'd like to buy it, bring it in right here." Joe waved

his hand expansively at an empty corner of the gym.

Max pulled away from the other man's embrace. "I'm sorry, Mr. Farnsworth," he said firmly. "It's not for sale." Then, looking around at all the expensive gear in sight, he asked curiously, "What do you want it for?"

"I gotta get in shape," explained Joe. "I'd like you to help me train. I'll pay you."

"Train?" Corkle slanted an eye toward the door. He wanted to get out of there; this kooky rich man's house was no place for a guy like Max Corkle.

"Yeah, train. And as soon as I'm ready I'd like you to get me a tryout with the Rams."

"I don't understand. What are you trying out for?"

"Quarterback," said Joe quietly.

"Quarterback?" Corkle's eyebrows shot up so fast they nearly knocked his cap off. Jeez, was this one a fruitcake! Edging to the door, Corkle tried to be diplomatic. "See, the thing is, Mr. Farnsworth, the thing is we already got a quarterback working with the team. Tom Jarrett. And we got a couple of pretty good backups—"

"You call Hodges good?" scoffed Joe, shaking his head in scorn.

"The point is, Mr. Farnsworth"—Corkle was edging a little faster—"we don't need a quarterback. Why don't you try some other team? What about the Oakland Raiders? They're pretty close to L.A. Give 'em a call and see what they say."

But Joe wasn't going for any of that. "I want to play quarterback, and I want to get in shape in time for the Super Bowl," he insisted. "How much would it cost me to get a tryout?"

Now Corkle was making openly for the exit. This guy wasn't playing with a full deck. "Mr. Farnsworth, no team wants a crazy trainer. And only a crazy trainer would arrange for you to try out as quarterback. So why don't you keep your money and I'll keep my job, and we'll keep this little . . . uh . . . misunderstanding to ourselves."

Joe sighed. He'd been afraid of this. What else could he expect? It was time to level with Max. On the face of the earth, the only man he could trust with the truth was Max Corkle. The problem was, how did he get him to believe it and deal with it?

Joe looked around. Except for the two guys moving the equipment and the guys up on the ladder, Max and he were alone in the vast ballroom.

"Wait," he said to Max. "Please wait."

To the guys on the ladders he yelled, "Take a lunch break," and to the moving men he said, "That's all right, you guys. I'll take care of that stuff."

In a minute or two, they were alone. Corkle and Pendleton, or, depending on how you looked at it, Corkle and Farnsworth. Corkle looked at it the second way, and with no favorable eye. He was antsy, suspicious, and eager to get his car on the other side of those hot-wired gates.

Sensing all of this, Joe took a deep breath. He'd done some difficult things in his time, but they'd been duck soup compared with this. How was he going to convince this guy, this old friend of Pendleton's who'd seen the smashed-up body and the ashes blowin' in the wind, that Joe Pendleton was alive and well and living in Leo Farnsworth? Max was the most straight-up guy that Joe had ever known, and Max believed in only what he could smell and see and touch. Max's philosophy was exactly that of the stray dog—if you couldn't eat it and you couldn't screw it, piss on it.

Where to begin?

"Uh, Max . . ." said Joe.

CHAPTER VIII

"Yes?" said Max cautiously and without enthusiasm.

"Look, what would you say if I told you that I was a professional football player?" asked Joe.

Max slitted his eyes. "What would *you* say if I told you I ran a conglomerate?" he retorted.

Joe tried another tack. "Max?"

"Yes?" sighed Corkle.

"You know how people die?"

Corkle looked around. There was nobody here but himself and this fruitcake. "Yeah. Why?" Out. He wanted out.

"And then . . . after they die they go to heaven?" Joe went on.

Heaven. Oh, sure. Better humor him. Otherwise he might call the security guards. "Well . . . I guess they do . . . if they're good. Why not?"

"You know how it works in heaven?" Joe persisted.

Yeah. You fly around on wings, playing a harp. Only this guy was flying around without wings. He was batty. "No. Not exactly." Why had Farnsworth sent for him? Had the keepers dropped the end of his chain?

"Probability and Outcome," said Joe solemnly.

"Probability and Outcome," Max repeated, nodding. He would have agreed if Farnsworth had said Abbott and Costello.

"Probability and Outcome," verified Joe.

Max took a deep breath. "No. I didn't know that,"

he said, and headed straight for the door. But Farnsworth was blocking him.

"Let's say that there's a Probability that some guy's gonna die," he explained. "An Escort from the guy's Way Station gets a signal and goes down and waits for the Outcome. Understand? If the guy dies, the Escort takes him back up to his Way Station and puts him in line for his final destination. You follow me?"

"Sure," said Corkle. He understood perfectly. L.A. was filled with weirdos like this one. All of them talked to God and traveled to Venus in flying saucers, and some of them went on murderous rampages. He slitted his eyes at Farnsworth again. Was this one the murderous kind? Nah, he seemed harmless enough for a hockey puck. The difference between Farnsworth and the old ladies with the tennis sneakers who yelled on the street was that Farnsworth was rich enough to have his secretary pick you out of the phone book and shlep you all the way to hell and gone up here so that Farnsworth could give you his rap about Escort angels. "Do you mind if I smoke?" he asked suddenly, pulling out a cigar.

"No. Go ahead. Now, let's say there's a new Escort. Really raw. He gets the signal, takes off, sees a guy, say, riding a bicycle into a tunnel and a car's coming the other way. Now, what he oughta do is wait for the Outcome. The Escort, I mean. But he's new, and he's so sure the guy is a goner that he figures why make him sit there and feel that car smash him up, so he pulls the guy out of there a few seconds early and takes him back up to his Way Station." Joe was really caught up in his explanation, and he felt he was finally getting through to Max.

"Uh . . . I need a match," said Corkle.

"That clock right there is a lighter." Joe pointed at the dragon on the mantel. It was one of Farnsworth's favorite additions to the house's decor. "This guy the Escort pulled up to the Way Station happens to be an athlete and he has these fantastic reflexes, and it turns out that he wouldn't have been hit by the car at all."

Thank God. The end of the story, thought Max. "How do you light this clock?" he asked, fiddling with it.

"You got to wind it," said Joe.

Corkle turned the winding key and a flame shot out of the dragon's mouth, nearly taking his eyebrows off. Joe showed him how to turn it down, and Corkle took a deep, healthful, invigorating, *sane* puff on his fifty-cent cigar.

"So," continued Joe, "the guy wasn't really dead. He woulda missed the car. His number wasn't up for years!" He beamed at Max triumphantly.

Years. The only years Max knew about were the ten years this story was taking. "Oh, hey! Look at the time!" he said with false brightness. "Is this lighter right?"

"I don't think so," said Joe. "And they're supposed to put him back into his body, but they can't, because it turns out he's been cremated. So they got to find another body to put him in. You understand?" Joe smiled at him hopefully.

Now Max was backing away across the long ballroom, with Joe following him closely, and smiling with all his teeth. "Yeah, but I'm just a trainer," he explained. "What you need is more like . . . a really good doctor."

The smile faded from Joe's face, and disappointment turned the corners of his mouth down. "Max, don't you understand what I'm trying to tell you?"

Corkle backed faster, grinning so as not to make Farnsworth mad. "Understand? Yeah, sure. That's a hell of a story."

"Max . . . Max . . ." Joe pleaded, holding out his hand. Then he caught sight of Mr. Jordan, watching him with sympathy. Mr. Jordan was standing on a brand-new six-hundred-dollar digital scale, which read out zero. "Oh, Mr. Jordan, I'm so glad to see you! I gotta get Farnsworth into shape for the Super Bowl, and I need to get Corkle here to help me."

Max looked up apprehensively. What new lunacy was this?

"Is there somebody else with us?" he asked, although he didn't really want the answer.

"This is Mr. Jordan," Joe said, pointing at nothing. "He runs the Way Station I was telling you about. Oh, yeah, you can't see him. You're still alive."

Corkle hated the sound of that "still." That was the most ominous syllable he'd ever heard. "You two guys probably got a lot to talk about, so I'll be on my way," he said heartily, making a slick move toward the door. "Goodbye and good luck."

"Wait a minute, Max." Joe begged.

"Tell him who you are, Joe," said Mr. Jordan gently.

But Joe was shaking his head in discouragement. "He's never going to believe me, Mr. Jordan. Can't *you* tell him everything that's happened? He's the only person I know who can get me a tryout with the Rams."

"You can make him believe you, Joe. Go on, tell him." Mr. Jordan's eyes glowed deeply. Their radiance put new spirit into Pendleton.

"Max, look at me," he ordered.

"Look, Mr. Farnsworth," Max began, determined to be out the gates in the next two minutes.

"I'm not Farnsworth. *I'm Joe Pendleton.*"

Corkle's jaw dropped and the cigar nearly fell out. He stared at Farnsworth. This guy didn't look or sound anything like Joe Pendleton. He was crazy! But, the eyes . . . there was something about those eyes. They were the exact color of Joe's, dark blue and very clear. Naw! What was he thinking of? Was Farnsworth's lunacy contagious?

"Don't you understand?" Joe pleaded. "This is just the body they stuck me into. Farnsworth was murdered

102

by his wife and private secretary. They drugged him and put him in the bathtub. But then I stepped into the body. I mean, it's not such bad material, but I gotta start trying to get it back in shape . . . Hey, Max, where you going?"

Corkle was heading for the exit, half on the run. "I don't wanna hear any more. I wanna get out of here, and I won't say a word to anybody!" he promised. "This will be just between you and me. It'll just be our little secret."

"Our little secret?" Joe called after him. "You mean, like what you told me about your older sister and the Coca-Cola salesman?"

Corkle stopped in his tracks. "How'd you know about that?" he demanded, thunderstruck.

"Or like how you really got that scar on the bottom of your tongue?" Joe pursued him.

"I never told that to anyone!" protested the bewildered Corkle, backing away in terror.

But Joe was relentless. "Or about what you did at your uncle's wedding?"

"No. No. You don't know me! Who told you these things?"

"Come here, Max." Suddenly, Joe's arm snaked out and caught the petrified Corkle around the neck in a headlock. "How about the first time I fixed your neck in that hotel in Pittsburgh?"

Trapped in the headlock, Corkle couldn't utter a sound, but his rolling eyes were still saying no.

"Say you believe me," demanded Joe. He gave Corkle's neck a jerk, as he always had when it was stiff. "Please tell me you believe me," he pleaded. "You gotta believe me." Joe searched his memory for more evidence. "Listen to me, Max," he said quietly. "They don't have a football team in heaven, so God couldn't make me first string." He whispered the words directly into Max's ear.

Max Corkle closed his eyes. "Oh, my God!" he moaned, trying to squirm out of the headlock. Those words . . . he'd spoken those words only to Joe Pendleton's ashes. How did this homicidal maniac get hold of them? Did he have the power to read Corkle's mind?

"He doesn't believe me, Mr. Jordan." Tears stung Joe's eyes and filled his throat. Corkle was not only his only chance, he'd been his only friend.

"Try a little music," suggested Mr. Jordan. "It's a great persuader."

Instantly, Joe released Corkle's neck and ran to the ballroom stage to get his saxophone.

Corkle moved his head gingerly from side to side, as though his neck were made of glass. Hey, it felt better! What do you know! The stiffness was gone. Suddenly, the notes of a soprano sax reached his ear. It was "Sweet Georgia Brown," or an approximate rendition thereof. Max winced. Every other note was wrong, and those were the identical notes that Joe Pendleton had always soured.

All of a sudden, everything clicked into place, like his neck. That cockeyed story about the bicycle and the tunnel, the athlete and the Escort and the Way Station. Joe Pendleton's eyes in another man's face. Those secrets that Farnsworth had no way of knowing, but that Joe had been privy to. All tied up by the terrible music.

Corkle turned around slowly. The tall guy was sitting on the stage, blowing lovingly into his sax. He was wearing the same dreamy expression that Joe always wore when he was into "a man and his music."

"Joe . . . Joe . . . you never could play that, Joe . . ." said Corkle. Overcome, he sank down on the steps of the stage. Alive! Joe was alive. It was crazy, sure. Maybe *he* was crazy for believing it, but he did. All at once and totally. He sank his head into his hands.

"Are you all right, Max?" Joe was patting his face, checking his pulse. Max merely nodded, unable to speak.

"Sisk! Sisk! Everett! Bentley!" yelled Joe, racing

out of the ballroom. "Whip up a couple of liver and whey shakes right away!" Triumphantly, gleefully, Joe ran back into the ballroom as the servants scattered.

"Max, I'm gonna play quarterback in the Super Bowl. Nothin' can change that if I got it comin' to me. Right, Mr. Jordan?"

"If, as you say, that's what you have coming to you, yes. Right." Mr. Jordan smiled.

Corkle looked around in mortal fear that he'd actually see something. "He still with us?" he asked Joe tentatively.

"He's right there. We gotta get in shape right away," urged Joe.

Now Corkle was coming back to life. He stood up, his reddish-gray hair bristling. "Don't you guys realize it's too late in the season?" he demanded. "How you gonna get in shape *that* fast?"

"Max, I still know all the moves. You just gotta help me get the body in shape."

But Max had had a rough afternoon, a little too rough for a guy of his age. His face turned a little pale, and he took a tottering step.

"Hey, Max, you don't look so hot. I'll get you that shake." He ran out of the room again and intercepted Sisk, who was carrying the concoction on a silver tray. Joe grabbed it up and was bringing it back when he saw Mr. Jordan standing in the hallway, looking at him.

"Thanks for the help, Mr. Jordan. Things are going great. Did you want to talk to me?"

"No." Mr. Jordan shook his head with a smile. "No, I can see that things are going great."

"Yeah, well, there's gonna be a lot of changes." Joe grinned. "You know what I'm going to do. I'm going to get Farnsworth a divorce. Thanks, Mr. Jordan. I gotta go. I gotta take care of Max."

"You do that, Joe." There were a few things that needed Mr. Jordan's attention, too, and he had to be getting on to them.

"I'd like to stay and talk to you, but I . . . sorry to rush off, Mr. Jordan." Carefully carrying the shake so that the brown froth on the top wouldn't spill over, Joe headed back for the ballroom. Mr. Jordan looked after him thoughtfully. This thing with Joe and Farnsworth had taken a new turn, and it was time to check out that heavenly computer again. Some permutations had arisen that had not been originally calculated for.

Meanwhile, the color had started to come back into Max's face, and his overloaded brain was beginning to accept the idea that had blown its circuits. Joe. It really *was* Joe Pendleton in that body of Farnsworth's. He believed it now. And, believing that, he also had to swallow the idea of there really being a life after death, and a Way Station and an Escort, and even a Mr. Jordan or a something that Joe called Mr. Jordan, and that evidently lived in that digital scale. And if there was a Mr. Jordan whom Joe could talk to, he could no doubt hear and see Max Corkle. And he no doubt had the kind of power that Max Corkle was badly in need of.

Taking off his cap and wiping at his brow, Max looked earnestly in the direction of the scale. "Uh . . . listen, Mr. Jordan," he began, feeling silly as hell. "Is that you? Mind if I talk to you for a minute?" He waited for lightning to strike, but nothing happened, and this oddly gave him more confidence.

Getting up from the steps, Max walked over to the scale and dropped his voice a little. "Sorry if I sounded off before. I want to apologize. I didn't mean to be disrespectful, you know. Look, here's the situation. You gotta help me talk Joe out of this, 'cause it's just not practical. I mean, Jesus—uh, forgive my language —if I go to the Rams and tell the owners that this polo-playing millionaire chairman of the board of Exo-Grey wants to be a quarterback, what the hell— sorry—do you think they'd say? They wouldn't even listen, they'd be laughing so hard.

"Besides, what for? Why does he need it? He's

rich now. He's much better off than when he was a football player with a bum knee. For years he's been trying to play that saxophone and he still can't do it. Not everything is possible, right? You know that. I can get him a tryout, I suppose, but Joe's just not in shape—I mean Farnsworth's not in condition—I mean, Joe's body— Oh, you know what I mean! The team would put him out of commission like that!" Max tried to snap his fingers but couldn't. They wouldn't snap. This talking to an invisible . . . something . . . was taking everything out of him.

Everett and Bentley, eavesdropping in the ballroom doorway, looked at each other in silence, shaking their heads. First Mr. Farnsworth was talking to mops. Now this oddly dressed stranger was holding a conversation with a scale. Either this house was haunted, or money makes you do very strange things. As Joe appeared with the shake, they glided off swiftly, with the invisibility that servants always develop.

"Hey, Max, who ya talkin' to?" Joe asked cheerfully.

Max jumped as though he'd been stung. "Your friend, Mr. Jordan," he said guiltily.

"Mr. Jordan? He's not there. Hey, Max, don't get crazy on me. Not now when I need you. Drink this. Here, take it, it won't poison you. We have to make our plans, starting now."

Reluctantly, averting his eyes from the brown foam on the top of the glass, Max took the liver shake. He gave one last, reproachful glance at the digital scale. Damn it, if you couldn't trust an angel, who *could* you trust?

CHAPTER IX

To build up Farnsworth's body and turn it into Rams' material took will, discipline, and money, all of which Joe had plenty of. Rising every morning at five, he ran. The estate provided lots of running room, uphill and down, flat track and rugged. After the first morning, when Joe had nearly been killed three separate times, the private security force, including the attack dogs, had been instructed to lay off the quickly moving figure in the warm-up suit. No teeth and no bullets. After a week, they got used to seeing Mr. Farnsworth streaking past them from any direction, waving "Hi." He was getting faster, too, and not puffing so much.

After coming in from his run, Joe would go directly to the ballroom, where his private gym waited, to work out, first with the barbells and then on the machines. With all the exercise machines in place, the ballroom had taken on the look of a mad scientist's laboratory. Weights and pulleys, handles and levers, benches fitted out to look like operating tables—Sisk would pass the ballroom with his eyes averted, and Julia wouldn't go anywhere near it; to her, it was as sinister and deadly as a minefield. Whatever Leo was doing in that place, hour after hour, day after day, Julia Farnsworth was convinced that it was part of some diabolical plot that would lead to her destruction.

Tony Abbott wasn't so sure. He had long since accepted the fact that Leo Farnsworth was mad; most likely the nose spray that had been intended to kill

Farnsworth had affected his brain. Actually, this played nicely into his and Julia's hands, although he couldn't yet figure out how. It might come to him, though. A crazy Farnsworth appeared less dangerous than a sane one, but even better would be no Farnsworth at all. But that came next.

The second part of the training program was for Joe to practice with a team. That was where the servants came in. When he outlined his plan to Sisk, and to Everett and Bentley, and to the chauffeur and the security guards and the maids, he was met with astonished silence. Play football? Run around the grounds catching and throwing and intercepting and blocking? Who, them? But when they saw the uniforms that Joe had had made up specially for them, they began to get into the spirit of it. After all, a little exercise never hurt anybody, and it beat polishing silver and ironing shirts.

Julia, still enmeshed in the conspiracy theory, now saw that conspiracy extending to her servants, so she spent much of the day locked in her bedroom, watching the scrimmages in the garden from her window, and wondering when the ax would fall. She whimpered a lot.

Tony, on the other hand, was busier and happier than ever. He had always handled a large portion of Mr. Farnsworth's Exo-Grey business. Before it used to be the donkey work, now it was executive-action stuff. More and more, he felt that he personally was becoming indispensable to the Exo-Grey board of directors and Leo Farnsworth was less and less necessary. Any minute now, he wouldn't be necessary at all . . . then pow! Right in the kisser . . . or keister, or whatever they called it when somebody became very, very dead very, very suddenly.

Even though Joe's days were geared to one thing only—preparation for the Rams tryout—his relationship with Betty Logan was deepening. Not that he had time for love. He was in bed and asleep every evening before ten. But in the long afternoons, when Joe ran plays over the grassy lawns, Betty would come and sit quietly on the sidelines. Sometimes she'd read a book, sometimes she'd work on her needlepoint. But whenever Joe completed a pass, he would look to her for approval. And always he'd meet that large, warm smile that made him feel so good.

When the practice sessions were over, and the rolling tea cart had trundled the silver bucket of Gatorade off the field, and the servants had gone to what they now called the "locker room" to shower and change, Joe and Betty would go for walks. Hand in hand, they'd walk through the formal gardens past the marble fountains and benches, through the rambling meadows, over little artificial streams and on bridle paths that cut through the woods of the estate. Sometimes they'd talk a mile a minute; at other times they'd be silent. But on every walk they exchanged little pieces of themselves, so that each one was now carrying a large part of the other deep inside.

"Do you think I'm crazy?" Joe asked her one day.

"Does it matter what I think?" She smiled.

"Yes."

"Does it matter if you're crazy?"

"No."

"I think you're crazy and I think you're wonderful. I think if the whole world were as crazy as you are, it would be a happier place to live in. And I think that I'm crazy, too, and it feels rather splendid, actually."

In the early evenings, Joe would curl up with the Rams' play book. Every day his arm was better, his coordination improved. Thank God that Farnsworth had a naturally long reach and two good knees. Joe was beginning to feel each muscle starting to coordinate with the rest. When they all worked together in response to his every unspoken command, then he'd be a football player again. He had faith.

He had faith, Betty had faith, the servants had no

idea what they were doing or why, but even they had faith. Only Max Corkle had little faith. He came every day to work with the "team" as it practiced, he saw Joe's passes getting longer and more expert, his legs moving fast, his feints and roll-outs improving, but still he had little faith.

"It's not going to work," he kept insisting whenever he and Joe had a few minutes alone. "It's not just that it's going to be tough. It's going to be more than tough, it's impossible! You're talking about playing with the Rams, but what you're actually doing is playing with a bunch of butlers. There's a world of difference between a team made up of maids and a team of professional football players."

As they walked back from the final scrimmage to the house, Corkle was still shaking his head. "It's never gonna happen, Joe. Here it is late December; the Super Bowl is only a week away. I haven't even spoken to them about a tryout yet, but I know what they're gonna say. Face it, Joe. It's never gonna happen."

Joe clapped Max on the shoulder. "Don't worry about it. It's all fixed. I took care of it myself." He grinned.

Corkle stopped on the path and looked up at Joe, astonishment written all over his craggy face. "*You* fixed it? How?"

"I bought the Rams," said Joe.

Even the loud boom of the sunset gun didn't penetrate Max Corkle's hearing. He stood frozen to the ground, saying over and over to himself, he bought the Rams. He bought the Rams. I don't believe it. He bought the Rams.

If Corkle couldn't believe it at first, he came to accept it in a relatively short time. But the news dropped on the team itself like a clap of thunder on a sunny day. One week from the Super Bowl, one week from playing the Steelers for the championship, and they'd been sold! Ed Figarello, the team's general manager, had some trouble getting enough order in the frenzied locker room so that he could be heard.

"I called you all together to talk to you about a very important matter . . . c'mon fellas, let's be quiet here. You probably all know by now that Leo Farnsworth bought the team. What you don't know is that Farnsworth wants to play quarterback."

The sound of forty male voices all shouting at once shook the locker-room ceiling and made the steel lockers vibrate.

"Are you kidding?" shouted a huge defensive lineman. "One week before the Super Bowl?"

"That's the way it is." Figarello nodded gloomily. "Mr. Farnsworth will be playing quarterback in Wednesday's scrimmage, at which time he and the coach will decide whether or not he's qualified for the job."

Forty necks swiveled at once and forty pairs of eyes sought out Tom Jarrett, who stood like a statue of granite, leaning against his locker. This wasn't news to him, what Figarello was telling the other guys. He'd already had a private conference with the outgoing owners, the coach, and the general manager. But he didn't look happy. His face was grim, and the muscles in his jaw stood out like boulders.

"And Mr. Farnsworth said," continued the manager, " 'Tell no one to hold back.' As a matter of fact, those were his very words. I quote: 'Tell no one to hold back. Let's play that scrimmage like it was the Super Bowl.' All right, fellas, let's play that scrimmage like the Super Bowl." He waited for the sudden murmur of excited voices to die down before he went on.

"Well, as for me, I welcome anybody that's got the guts to get out there and play with you fellas and cut the mustard. Mr. Farnsworth's not afraid of the blood in your eyes. He wants you to hit. And hit hard. Now, take him at his word, fellas. Hit him hard." Satisfied that his message had gotten across, Figarello stepped down from the bench and left the locker room to allow the team to talk it over among themselves.

"Let's give him a shot. Okay?"

"We sure will," came a threatening voice from the rear of the locker room.

"We're going to look like a bunch of assholes," moaned another.

"Let's kill him," suggested Gorman. Six feet seven inches tall and weighing two-seventy-five, the defensive tackle from Watts was the most dangerous member of the team. His favorite sound was the sickening snap of a broken bone—one of the offense's bones—and when he brought his man to the ground, it was generally in a smear.

"Let's not kill him," countered Kowalsky, the second defensive tackle. Kowalsky had been raised in a family where he was the youngest of eleven children. He'd had to fight for his life daily, and it had turned him into an effective killing machine. Six feet five and two-sixty-eight, Kowalsky's chief joy in life, next to eating and waitresses, was felling a man, like a lumberjack with a power saw. "Let's not kill him. Let's just make him lose interest."

"Yeah, right."

"We won't kill him, we'll just make him lose interest."

"Ha, ha, ha, ha. Make him lose interest, that's good."

"Yeah, that's a good one."

Kowalsky's suggestion had found favor with his teammates, and they put their heads together in a huddle, to develop a few plays that this new quarterback would definitely not have the signals for.

Joe sensed their hostility as soon as he came into the locker room to get his ankles taped and to climb into uniform. Not that he blamed them. He'd expected some of it; it was only natural, since he was the man responsible for disrupting the team only a week before the Super Bowl. Still, the quality and quantity of the resentment took him by surprise. Secretly, he'd harbored the smallest wish that they'd welcome him, for old times' sake, even if they didn't know there *was* an old times' sake. Corkle looked worried, too. He knew the guys were up to something, even if he couldn't tell Joe specifically what.

"Get rid of the ball," was all Max could advise Joe in a muttered undertone as Joe ran out on the field. "They're gonna cream you."

They got him with the very first play, since they weren't in any mood to screw around. Joe, with the Rams' play book in his head, had called a relatively uncomplicated opening offense, just to get the ball moving down the field, but the defense caught him totally by surprise.

Before the ball had even been snapped, Kowalsky and Gorman came surging over the line illegally, a pair of angry-faced amphibious vehicles. The offense parted like the Red Sea, and the two defensive tackles surged all over Joe, bringing him down and grinding him into the turf.

So this is how they want to play it, thought Joe, as he came to. He sat up groggily and checked his limbs to make sure that nothing visible to the naked eye was broken. Then he tried to stand up and finally made it. He was, by some miracle, still in one piece.

Gorman and Kowalsky were certain that this was *it* for Leo Farnsworth. Now the nice rich man would go away and mind his own business and let them get on with their work, getting ready for the Super Bowl against Pittsburgh.

But Joe had other ideas. If he couldn't outweigh them, he could outplay them. Now was his chance to find out exactly what he had accomplished with Leo Farnsworth's body, and what he could accomplish against professionals. He could see the way the land lay.

On the second play, Joe took the snap from center

and dropped back quickly, looking for his receivers. From the corner of his eye he could see Gorman and Kowalsky surging toward him again, more like a trucker's convoy than flesh and blood. Just as they were about to reach him, Joe threw a short turn in pass to his tight end and ducked. Gorman and Kowalsky collided. You could hear the mighty thunk of their helmets crashing together throughout the Coliseum, and the impact of their mammoth bodies hitting the turf shook the stadium. It was the end of the age of the dinosaurs.

When Gorman came to, stumbling groggily to his knees, he could see Farnsworth running in place on his own thirty-yard line. Kowalsky was still out, an inert mass sprawled on the ground.

"Where did he learn that?" muttered Gorman to himself with a dawning respect. He shook his head to see how many of his teeth were loose.

On the next play, Joe completed a forty-yard pass and the Rams began to look at each other. What the hell? This guy knew how to play football! From that minute on, they started to play *with* him, not against him. They were curious to see what he could do. The offensive line began to protect him, the defense to answer his plays rather than attacking him indiscriminately. It was starting to look like football out there.

It was truly astounding. Here was a guy of at least thirty-three or -four, with no pro training that anybody had ever heard of, a guy who was known only as a shark in the ocean of industry, an eccentric millionaire, and he could play football! Not that piddling touch football, the rich man's game, but bone-crushing, soul-grinding professional ball. He was fast on his feet, his eye was accurate and his arm strong. Most of all, he seemed to know just where to place that ball on every play. At the line of scrimmage, he was calling audibles left and right, confusing the defense.

Up in the stands, just below the press box, the former

owner of the Rams watched the play and ground his teeth.

"My team! My team! That son of a bitch got my team!" he growled.

"What kind of pressure did he use, Milt?" asked Bradley.

"I asked for sixty-seven million dollars, and he said okay."

"Ruthless bastard!"

"What the hell is the matter with you guys?" the former owner yelled down to the field as he saw Farnsworth carrying the ball deep into defense territory. "Play football!"

"Your heart, Milt!" cautioned Bradley.

It wasn't only Milt's heart that was in danger. The head coach, watching from the sidelines, was also feeling the strain. He was almost incoherent, his face turning apoplectic purple. "I don't believe it . . . he can't . . . you can't do that if you're not a professional . . . How did he . . . Not possible . . . I've been coaching for eleven years and I've never . . ."

"Yeah, well," said Max Corkle sympathetically. "It could be luck."

Down on the fifty-yard line, in the best seats, sat Oppenheim and Renfield, president and senior vice-president of Exo-Grey. They watched their chairman of the board completing pass after pass, with mingled alarm and exasperation on the part of Oppenheim and downright admiration from Renfield.

"Now, Henry, he's an eccentric. We've always known that about Leo Farnsworth," said Renfield.

"Do you call it eccentric to pay sixty-seven million dollars for a football team that has a book value of nineteen?" fumed Oppenheim. "And have you any idea what our stock opened at this morning? Fourteen! Three weeks ago, shares were selling at fifty-six. This morning—fourteen. Is that what you call eccentric? I call that just plain insanity!"

Joe stood up as the whistle blew for the last time.

It was over. He'd done it. He'd shown the Rams he could do it. What was most important of all, he'd shown *himself* he could do it—start from scratch with a body not even his, and bring that body into the kind of shape that could go up successfully against— and with—some of the best football players in the world. The tryout had been a success, not because the Rams had accepted him, but because Joe had finally accepted himself. Because what he hadn't told Corkle, what he hadn't even admitted out loud to himself, was this: Joe wanted the Rams to win the Super Bowl even more than he wanted to quarterback them. If this tryout had proved to him that he wasn't up to his own high standards, he would have let it go. Even though he owned the team, he would have cheered from the sidelines, not from the benches.

He could see the other men—his teammates now— looking at him with respect. Without that respect, they weren't a team. He would have been no more than an intruder, and he would have screwed them up badly. As it was, he hadn't made it easy for them, and he was sorry for that now.

Somebody had owed him this shot at the championship, and he'd been determined to collect it, no matter what. Now, stripping off his uniform and heavy pads in the locker room, Joe realized that he'd been . . . well . . . wrong. He'd been thinking about himself and only himself. Not the Rams, but Joe Pendleton. He was glad it had worked out okay, but he was seeing things a little differently now.

As the other players were obviously collecting the nerve to come up and rap with their new owner, Joe smiled to himself. Funny, he hadn't thought he had anything more to learn. But he'd been wrong. Who taught me that? he wondered. Mr. Jordan? Betty? Just being in another man's body? Whatever or whoever it was, it had been a valuable lesson, and he was glad to learn it.

Julia Farnsworth ground her teeth together as she looked out of her bedroom window. How much more could mere flesh and blood stand? First, he doesn't die. Then he starts acting really crazy. Next, he decides he wants to be a football player, and he tears my ballroom apart and brings in a lot of smelly equipment and that crazy old man who talks to scales, and he takes all the servants away and makes them chase a ball all over my gardens, and they've wrecked the roses. Then he tells me he wants a divorce. Then he doesn't die again. Then he starts hanging around with that skinny, frizzy-haired girl with the English accent.

And now look at him!

"Look!" she shrieked at Tony, waving one hand covered in diamonds and fingernail polish. "Look at that! He's brought the whole goddamned football team here. And he's posing with them." She chewed viciously on an expensive nail.

Tony looked out of the window. On the lawn below, a party of men and women was strolling in the gardens, heading for the lovely teahouse that was a *House Beautiful* feature of the estate. The sound of conversation and laughter drifted up through the languid air. Among them, Leo Farnsworth was smiling and acting the grand host, while Everett and Bentley carried trays of refreshments around.

"No, dearest," said Tony soothingly. "See all the older men? And see how skinny some of the younger ones are? And see all the women? That's not a football team. Those are the ecology groups that Exo-Grey is funding."

But Julia was beyond listening to soothing words. "He's getting ready to spring some kind of trap," she gritted. "This whole thing—the football-team gag, the divorce crap, the ecology shit—it's all part of a plot. The only thing he hasn't announced to the newspapers is the divorce. And once he does, I'm gonna be the first person they'll suspect when we kill—" Here she broke off as Abbott's palm clamped her jaws together.

"Dearest," cooed Tony. "Perhaps I'm just being silly, but I'd feel so much better if you . . . Why, Julia, your eyes are glazing!" He took his hand away. "Are you mad at me? Have I offended you?"

Julia was breathing hard, her shoulders heaving and her eyes bugging out of her head. "Don't put your hand over my mouth again!" she warned him.

"All right," pouted Tony. "But you used to like it."

"Listen to me. If we don't do something right away, we're gonna lose it all. Every penny. I should have my head examined for signing that prenuptial agreement. I'll end up with an allowance and some wardrobe, and you'll be fired without references."

"We'd still have each other." Abbott attempted to put his arms around Julia, but she dug him so sharply in the ribs with her elbow that he doubled over, his toupee slipping down.

"Not after he brings charges against us for the last two murder attempts," hissed Julia. "He must have collected evidence—no, don't you do it!" she snarled as Tony's hand rose automatically toward her mouth. "Just . . . put . . . your . . . hand . . . right . . . back . . . down . . . at . . . your . . . side. . . . Because . . . if . . . you . . . put . . . it . . . over . . . my . . . mouth . . . you'll . . . be . . . missing . . . a . . . *palm!*"

Tony had never seen her so . . . convincing. "Dearest, don't be upset," he pleaded. "It's just a habit. I didn't even know my hand was up." He lowered it with an elaborate gesture. "See? Down it goes, darling."

She was hysterical, but she was right. It was time to put an end to Farnsworth, not only because he was in a position to get them both but also because he was running his five-hundred-million-dollar fortune into the ground. Take away sixty-seven million dollars spent on a bunch of two-ton bruisers in shoulder pads and what did you have? Admittedly, a lot, but not when so much of it was in Exo-Grey stock, and Exo-Grey stock was plummeting. At the rate Leo was going, there would hardly be enough to keep Tony and Julia in the style to which they'd become accustomed. Not to mention the millions he was pouring into what that tart from Tigglesworth kept calling "the environment." Speaking of whom, wasn't that girl down there right now, smiling at her group of followers and making one of those radical speeches that kept Farnsworth writing those checks? Yes, it was she; Tony could recognize her by that cloud of yellow hair. He had to admit she looked like a pre-Raphaelite painting he'd priced for Farnsworth once, an angel by Burne-Jones. Grrrrrr. He really hated her, and one of the fringe benefits of offing Farnsworth would be getting rid of Miss Goody-Two-Shoes there. Just look at the way Farnsworth was ogling her. Now they were holding hands and moving away from the others, down a winding path into the wilder part of the gardens. He'd bet fifty shares of Exo-Grey that they were heading for the wishing well.

"It all depends on what kind of defense they're gonna throw at you," Joe was explaining as they walked slowly through the late-afternoon sunshine to the wishing well. "I'm glad you played hockey. It makes it a lot easier to talk to you." He stopped at a flowering bush and plucked off a sprig of scented blossoms. Awkwardly, he stuck it in her curly hair, aiming for behind her ear, but missing. He'd never put a flower in a girl's hair before.

I'll wager he's never put a flower in a girl's hair before, thought Betty, and the thought warmed her. He was so funny and endearing, this man so tall she had to tilt her head way back to look at him.

"Hey, you wanna make a wish?" Joe was standing now at the wishing well, basking in the warmth of Betty's smile. When she tilted her head like that to look up at him, he felt twelve feet tall and very powerful.

"Yes, I'd like that."

"Okay," said Joe, and dug into his pocket, coming up with a fifty-cent piece. Deftly, he performed the thumb palm, making the coin disappear, and pulling it out of the scented fluff of her hair. With a bow, he presented her with the half dollar.

"You're so clever," laughed Betty. She closed her eyes and wished hard, but oddly enough, for a girl who was so good with words, the wish came wordlessly to her. It was more a feeling than a wish, and it encompassed Joe's continued well-being as well as their continued happiness. Now, why did I wish that? she wondered to herself as she dropped the coin into the well. It fell way, way down and she had to wait for the splash. The well was quite deep.

"Do you think it's silly?" asked Joe. "Me trying to be a football player?"

Betty smiled up at him again, her eyes bright blue with happiness. "I think you can do anything you want to," she said. "Absolutely anything."

Joe hesitated, almost afraid to hear her answer to his next question. "You mean . . . because I'm a big wheel at Exo-Grey?" He still felt insecure on that point . . . was Betty in love with Leo Farnsworth, with his power and money, or with the man inside the body?

"No," said Betty, shaking her head with certainty. "It's got nothing to do with that. It's because you're not afraid."

A great weight lifted itself off Joe's chest, and he felt like flying. "What is there to be afraid of?" he asked her happily. "You know the only thing I'm afraid of?"

Betty looked up at him, her face serious and questioning.

Joe wasn't sure how to put this into words. "I'm afraid," he said slowly and very softly, "of how I'd feel if I couldn't be with you." It was the first time in his life he'd said anything like that to a woman, or revealed his vulnerability. On the other hand, he'd never felt vulnerable with a woman before, and he wasn't sure of the rules.

"Well, then," said Betty brightly, her eyes twinkling with mischief, "there's nothing to be afraid of, is there?"

Joe's heart felt so full that his next words came out all in a rush, tumbling over themselves to get to Betty's ears. "This might sound crazy to you, but how would you feel about marrying me?"

Betty stood silent for a long moment while she listened to what her heart had to tell her. It would be complicated, she knew that. This man was not the sort she'd always had in the back of her mind as a mate. He was different. Haunted, almost. Sometimes she had the clear impression that there were two of him, two Leo Farnsworths in that body, one that the rest of the world saw, and one that only she had knowledge of. She knew, too, that he had turned his back on everything in his earlier life—his position, his possessions, even his wife. How could she be certain he wouldn't turn his back on her someday? She looked up at him, into his clear blue eyes. Those eyes. They could never lie, she thought. He had the clearest, truest eyes in all the world.

"It doesn't sound crazy to me," she said softly.

It was going to happen, all of it, Joe thought with a great surge of exultation. He was going to win his game and marry his girl and live as simply and as close to reality as he knew how. . . .

"I'd like to come . . ." he began. "Could I come to Pagglesham? After the game I'd like to get out of here, see what it's like in Pagglesham—" He broke off as something caught his attention.

Past the wishing well, over the green of the garden shrubbery, standing against a tree, Joe saw the Escort. All at once, a feeling of apprehension filled him, and his fear was reflected in his eyes.

"What is it?" cried Betty anxiously as she saw his expression change. "What are you looking at?"

"Look, can you wait right here a second? I won't be a minute." Joe looked urgently again at the Escort, who stood watching him, obviously waiting for him.

Betty turned toward the shrubbery, but she saw nothing, nobody. Her anxiety increased. Was he all right?

"Let me come with you," she said.

But Joe shook his head hurriedly. He reached over and grabbed her by her shoulders, looking into her face with an urgency she could not deny. "I'll be right back. I'll be right back. Please wait here for me."

Nodding wordlessly, Betty cast her eyes down so that she wouldn't have to watch him go. She was troubled by his sudden agitation; was he in some difficulty? Sometimes he seemed so . . . vulnerable. And so alone. As though whatever he had to do, nobody could help him with.

Striding across the lawn, Joe moved quickly to the tree beside which the Escort stood. He seemed to be grayer than ever, pale and ashen, and his mouth had a tight, pinched look.

"What do *you* want?" demanded Joe brusquely.

The Escort took one step forward, then he cleared his throat and looked Joe straight in the eye. "I'm sorry, Mr. Pendleton," he said in a clear but uneasy voice, "but I'm afraid you can't use Mr. Farnsworth's body any longer."

"What are you talking about?" gasped Joe.

"Just what I said. Your time is up."

CHAPTER X

"Now, wait one minute!" said Joe in a strangled voice. "Didn't you tell me . . . didn't you *promise* me that I was going to get to the Super Bowl?"

The Escort's face showed a fleeting sympathy, which he forced himself to suppress. Escorts did not get personally involved. "All I know is that whatever you're going to do, it won't be with Mr. Farnsworth's body."

"Why not?" demanded Joe.

"It wasn't meant to be," the Escort replied in a distant voice.

"*Why not?*"

The Escort's composure crumpled. "Don't keep saying 'why not?' " he pleaded. "The point is—"

"The point is that you think I'm going to go on paying for *your* mistake," shouted Joe.

"Look, Mr. Pendleton," the Escort replied stiffly, "you haven't much time. And I suggest—"

"*I* suggest that you go back and tell Mr. Jordan that I want to talk to him. We're gonna settle this thing once and for all. I want to straighten this mess out right away. And get out of here!" he said angrily. "You're bad news."

His feelings hurt, the Escort dematerialized.

Adrenalin still coursing through him, Joe almost ran back to find Betty. As soon as she saw his face, some of his anxiety communicated itself to her. She didn't even have a name for her fear, but she leaped up from the stone bench and called out, "What's wrong?"

"Ah . . . nothing important," lied Joe. "Just something I gotta straighten out." He was beginning to feel a sense of loss—loss and hopelessness.

"There is something wrong!" Betty cried sharply. "Tell me what's wrong!" She peered into his face, trying to read his expression.

"No. No." Joe shook his head. "I was just thinking ..." He touched her shoulder, then his hand moved to her chin, cupping it, keeping her eyes locked to his. "You have to believe one thing, Betty. We . . . we got a great life ahead, you and me. Nobody's gonna take that away from us." His eyes devoured her face, her hair, and went back to her eyes again, which were now a troubled gray.

"Why are you looking at me like that?" she said, gripped by fear.

"I'm . . . I'm just memorizing your face. I want to memorize everything about you, so . . . no matter what happens . . . I won't forget you."

"Forget me! What's going to happen? Please, Joe . . .!"

Joe touched her soft cheek gently with his finger. "Nothing's gonna happen," he told her huskily. "You'd never forget me, either, would you?" His eyes begged hers.

"No," she said simply, drowning in her fear. Once again she sensed the strangeness of this man, the aloneness. She looked deeply into his eyes, as if she could read their future in them, but they were clouded, opaque.

"I mean . . ." said Joe, searching for words to make her understand what he knew she could never understand, ". . . the thing you said you saw in me. You said it was something in my eyes. Remember?"

"Yes, I remember," Betty whispered.

"Well," said Joe, groping for the right phrases, "if someday somebody came up to you . . . and he acted like he's seen you before . . . he might even be a football player . . . you'd notice that same thing. I mean . . . even if you only thought you did . . . you'd give him a chance, wouldn't you? He might be a good guy —" He broke off, unable to continue.

I'm losing him, thought Betty in panic. I'm losing him and I don't know why. "I don't understand what you're talking about," she said hopelessly.

Joe rested his hand on her hair for a minute, feeling its springy life and warmth. His face was sad, very sad and remote. The happiness that had been there only a short while ago was drained away now, hopelessness taking its place.

"Oh, I'm just acting a little crazy, that's all. Don't pay me any mind." He tried to smile at her, but it was a dismal failure.

Side by side, without speaking or touching, they walked through the garden and back to the house. Betty was possessed by the awful feeling that this was the last time she would ever see him. She couldn't shake it off; it was a premonition so strong that it made her shiver. Soon, too soon, they reached the house, where the long blue Daimler limousine stood waiting to take her home.

Suddenly, Joe wrapped his arms around her slim body and pulled her to him in a long kiss. She clung to him as if she would never let him go, and his lips and hers melted into one. Her body seemed to dissolve into his, as if he were trying to mingle their souls. At last he let her go, but she pulled his head down to hers for one last kiss. Last kiss, Betty thought. Now why did that occur to me, *last* kiss?

"I'll call you in a little while," said Joe as he helped her into the back seat of the limo.

"We've got a lot to talk about." Betty held tightly to his hand; she didn't want to let it go.

"We've got a lot to talk about," he agreed, closing the door of the car gently. He stood watching it down the driveway until he couldn't see it any more. But the memory of the pain and fear in her eyes was still imprinted on his brain.

Turning around, he saw Mr. Jordan, silhouetted in

a halo of setting sunlight, his eyes holding Joe's mutely. Joe opened his mouth to speak, to protest, to rage, but he closed it again. He was trapped in his feeling of helplessness, of events too powerful for him to control. When Mr. Jordan turned and silently moved off, Joe followed him.

Mr. Jordan led the silent Joe back through the gardens to the wishing well where he'd asked Betty to marry him. There Mr. Jordan turned, and the two confronted each other.

Tony Abbott, carrying a rifle with a telescopic sight, walked quickly into Julia Farnsworth's bedroom. Julia sat at her tulip-skirted dressing table, brushing out her thick mane of hair. Tony took his position at the open window. His eyes scanned the grounds. At the flagpole, Sisk and Bentley stood ready to lower the flag at sunset, as they did daily, while Everett manned the cannon. Where was Farnsworth? Abbott leaned out and looked around.

There he was, at the wishing well. He was gesturing wildly and talking to . . . Abbott squinted to get a better view . . . to absolutely nobody. No question about it. Farnsworth was totally bananas. The world would be a better place without him. Exo-Grey would be a better place without him. Julia's bed would be a better place without him. Tony Abbott raised the rifle to his shoulder.

"Why? *Why?*" Joe yelled desperately. "Why now, when everything's perfect? After all we've gone through, how can you expect me to give up Farnsworth now?"

"I'm sorry, Joe," said Mr. Jordan. He looked sorry, but determined.

Balling his hands into fists, Joe raised them to heaven in appeal. "You promised me I was going to get to the Super Bowl. Didn't you? Didn't you promise?"

"That is true," said Mr. Jordan gently. "If it is meant to be."

Joe backed off, shaking his head wildly. "I'm not leaving!"

"I'm sorry," Mr. Jordan said again.

"I'm not leaving!"

"Joe," Mr. Jordan pointed out, "it was you yourself who asked for a temporary arrangement."

"Look, I never went back on a deal in my life, Mr. Jordan. But I'm doing it now. I won't go." Stubborn resolve had turned Joe's blue eyes a darker color, almost navy, and his chin stuck out as if it could battle heaven and win.

"Your destiny is not in my hands," said Mr. Jordan, opening his hands to show them empty of Joe's destiny. "Please, Joe, don't make it more difficult."

But Joe was backing away again, unwilling to listen. "I'm not making it more difficult. I'm just not gonna go."

"You must abide by what is written," insisted Mr. Jordan in that same gentle voice.

Shaking his head insistently, Joe continued to back away. "I'm not going to go. You can't make me and nobody else can." Then, agonized, he cried out from his heart, "She loves me, Mr. Jordan!"

At the precise instant in eternity that Everett fired off the sunset gun, Tony Abbott pulled the trigger of the rifle. The rifle's crack was swallowed up in the sound of the cannon, but the body of Leo Farnsworth staggered, mortally wounded, spun around, and fell, deep, deep, deep into the icy waters of the wishing well.

Joe Pendleton, wearing his gray track suit and carrying his saxophone, walked beside Mr. Jordan down the cloud road leading to the Way Station.

"There is a plan, Joe. Don't be afraid. There is a reason for everything. There is always a plan, Joe. You mustn't be afraid."

But Joe was afraid. In his mind's eye he could see the blue and gold, the softness and loveliness of Betty, and he was deeply afraid that whatever arms were to be his would never hold her close, that whatever lips would be assigned to him would never kiss her. He had lost Betty Logan, and nothing could ever make up for it. Not if he lived another thousand lives.

"Oh, Bentley," called Tony Abbott. "Have you seen Mr. Farnsworth?"

Bentley closed the door of the master suite behind him. The bed had not been slept in. "No, sir, I haven't."

"Ah," said Tony. "Well, then, I shall just have to keep looking. Toodle-oo."

Max Corkle came through the ballroom door. The gym, which always contained Joe working out on the machines, now contained only the machines. Silent. Empty.

"Joe? You in here? Joe?"

Betty sat alone in her hotel room, fear gnawing at her insides, her head spinning with conflicting thoughts. Days. It had been days since he'd promised to call her and hadn't. And he'd acted so strangely, spoken so wildly! She tried to recall his exact words, but her emotions were too conflicting for her to think clearly. Something about not forgetting each other, that she did remember. And about his eyes . . . And some gibberish that she hadn't understood about a football player and being good to him and giving him a chance. Where was he? She was certain that he was in deep trouble, but of what description she had no idea. In trouble and alone, of that she was sure. Isolated from her, unable to reach her. She didn't feel deserted; Betty never doubted for a minute that he would have called her if he could have.

She picked up the telephone; she'd call him! No, she

thought as she dropped the receiver back on its cradle. No, that was unwise. He was still a married man, she laughed bitterly, even if he was her fiancé. And she knew in her heart that whatever trouble he was in, nobody could help him, not even she. No, she'd wait. As she'd promised him she would. She'd wait and she wouldn't forget him. Or the look in his eyes.

Eventually, of course, the police had to be called in, and Leo Farnsworth, multimillionaire industrialist and owner of the Los Angeles Rams, was reported missing. No note, no ransom demand, no sign of anything disturbed, no clothing taken from the closets (the police officers who searched Farnsworth's clothes closets came out in shock; that Farnsworth guy must have thought that every day was Halloween); no withdrawals from his checking accounts—in short, vanished without a trace.

The wire services picked up the story from the L.A. *Times* and flashed it all over the country: MILLIONAIRE MISSING! NO WORD YET ON LEO FARNSWORTH, INDUSTRIALIST AND SPORTSMAN, and, a day later, MILLIONAIRE'S DISAPPEARANCE STILL BAFFLES POLICE. This didn't make the police look good or feel happy; when the directors of Exo-Grey telephone the Governor of the state and the Mayor of the city and every Congressman with a constituency outside Watts, then somebody had better come up with something and that something had better be right.

Exo-Grey was in a turmoil, and Oppenheim had three lawyers working around the clock to find a loophole in the company's charter that would give him the right to call an immediate election and vote Leo Farnsworth out, or better yet, dead. Meanwhile, the company had put up a twenty-thousand-dollar reward for information leading to the whereabouts of Leo Farnsworth, and Tony Abbott had convinced Julia to double it. She fought tooth and bitten nail, but he managed to persuade her that staying in bed all day and pretending to cry was only half a convincing show. After all, the place was crawling with cops; it was a little early to be putting on black and calling the undertakers.

Lieutenant Griswold ("Gus") Krim of the L.A.P.D. had been assigned to the case and had picked detectives Peters and Conway to assist him. Krim was a pragmatic man, the kind who wore both belt and suspenders, and he liked neat cases in which there was only one suspect, who confessed shortly after being apprehended. Krim liked his *t*'s crossed and his *i*'s dotted, and all loose ends tied up in a bow. His favorite moment in any case was filing away the report in the drawer marked "Solved."

And the Leo Farnsworth case was a pain in the ass, and no mistake. Not only was every person of influence west of Beverly Hills leaning on him hard, there was no body, no evidence, and not a single clue. The man might have vanished into thin air or fallen down a well. There were four armed security police on the Farnsworth estate, not to mention every piece of electronic detection, surveillance, and preventive equipment sold outside the CIA, and the man seemed to have vanished in broad daylight. The dogs hadn't barked, and the guards had seen nothing.

Another thing that bugged him about the case was the number of people involved. Krim remembered vaguely that in English murder mysteries the butler always did it, and here were about fifteen goddamn butlers! Not to mention a wife, a secretary, and, it would seem, a girlfriend. As for motive, money aside, Farnsworth was well known to be a son of a bitch of the purest ray serene; everybody hated him, although nobody would admit it.

Was it a murder or was it a kidnapping? Or was it one of those cooked-up cases involving heavy insurance where the "widow" turns up in Buenos Aires five years later, arm in arm with the "deceased"? Krim had nothing to go on but an incipient ulcer, which twinged whenever he had a suspicion. The goddamn thing was biting all the time now; it was attempting to eat its way right through Krim's old blue suit.

Krim's phone had been jumping off the hook with pressure from above, and he chewed on a Tum now as he held the receiver at least two inches away from his ear. Conway could hear an angry blast of noise coming from the telephone.

"I'm telling you what I told the Mayor, Your Highness," winced Krim. "By the end of the week, we'll crack this case." At last he was able to hang up, and he growled at his assistant as he slammed the phone down.

"Another Arab. That son-of-a-bitch Farnsworth was into everything. And he's vanished. Conway, I cannot tell you what a schmuck I'm going to look like if we don't come up with something."

Conway shook his head in sympathy. They couldn't even come up with the FBI to help them until a ransom demand was made.

Inside the Rams' locker room, Figarello, Judson, and Corkle sat in bewildered gloom.

"I don't understand it," said the head coach for the tenth time, shaking his head in confusion.

Figarello, the general manager, shrugged. "Who knows? A guy comes, he buys the team, trains for the game—and takes off. He's the craziest nut I've ever had to deal with."

But Judson kept shaking his head. "He wasn't fooling around," he said glumly. "If he was alive, he'd be here."

Corkle didn't say a word; he didn't trust himself to speak. But he agreed with Judson. If Joe were alive, nothing could keep him from the Coliseum. But then, Joe had been dead before and look what happened. He came back. Are ya comin' back, Joe? he asked silently.

133

Are ya up there somewhere, maybe with Mr. Jordan? Aw, Joe, if only I could help.

Julia Farnsworth kept to her bedroom because it was the only place where it was safe to chew out Tony Abbott. She hadn't let up on him for days. Policemen were swarming all over the grounds, and Leo's body was right there in the well, for anybody to find.

"Nobody will look there," Tony assured her.

"How do you know?" she snarled.

"People think he's been kidnapped. They won't find him."

"Let's hope so!" hissed Julia. "Fool!" she added, to ease her feelings a little.

"I'm telling you," Tony argued, "they'll never find the body." He was getting very tired of hanging around this nest of tulips, but it was hardly safe to leave Julia alone. She was always unpredictable, but these days—! And with the servants so edgy, too.

"How can you be so sure?" she pressed him. "What makes you think that? Why didn't you shoot him someplace where we could have buried the body?"

"How are they going to find him at the bottom of a well?" demanded Tony in exasperation. "I'm telling you, don't worry, they'll never find him!"

But Julia was thinking now, picking at the pattern on the sheets with her long nails, her eyes narrowed. "It's very simple," she announced suddenly. "We'll have to close the house, send the servants away, and get a long rope . . ."

"But what about my back?" wailed Tony.

"I forgot about your goddamn back! Now we'll *never* get him out! Why didn't you shoot him someplace convenient? What makes you think they won't find him?" She was on the accusation merry-go-round again, and Tony groaned, longing to jump off.

"Are you asking me to believe, Miss Logan, that

Leo Farnsworth asked you to marry him?" demanded Lieutenant Krim.

Betty sat stiffly on the Naugahyde chair in the lieutenant's dingy downtown office. "Yes," she said in a quiet, steady voice. "He was going to get a divorce. And when I left, he said he'd call me. But something must have happened to him."

"How do you know that, Miss Logan?" asked Krim sharply.

Betty looked at the detective earnestly. "Because he didn't call me. And he would have kept his word if he could have."

Krim exchanged a quick glance with Conway, who raised one eyebrow significantly. "Well, thank you very much for coming down and giving us this information, Miss Logan," he said. The girl stood up uncertainly, smoothing down her skirt with a nervous hand.

"And, just as a formality," added Krim, opening the door for Betty, "let us know if you're planning to leave town, will you?"

"Yes. Of course I will." She stopped in the doorway, longing to ask questions, to beg for any scrap of information the police might have in their possession, but she thought better of it and left silently.

Krim closed the door after her and sighed as he sat down at his desk again. "Well," he told Conway, "that makes her the last person to see Farnsworth."

"The wife mention a divorce?" asked Conway.

The lieutenant shook his head. "Nope. Nobody did."

Conway smiled wryly. "Sounds like the oldest story in the world," he commented.

Krim shrugged. "What story is that?" He'd heard so damn many of them.

"Mr. Jordan! Mr. Jordan!" The Escort was out of breath, he had hurried so. "We've just been alerted. It's time for Mr. Pendleton to return."

"That's good news, Joe. You're going back." Mr. Jordan smiled.

"Can I be Farnsworth again?" pleaded Joe.

"Whatever is right for you . . . that's what will happen."

CHAPTER XI

To Detective Lieutenant Griswold ("Gus")
Krim, the "other woman" was always the prime suspect
in a murder, and Betty Logan's open face and straight-
forward manner were the clinchers—anybody who
looked that innocent just had to be guilty. He had her
tailed back to her motel, and he opened a file on her,
with round-the-clock surveillance and a close check
into her background. Krim was certain that she was
lying.

By Super Bowl day, Max Corkle was convinced
that Joe was dead. He was used to the boy's eccentricities, but this was carrying things too far. The
Super Bowl was Joe's only reason for having gone
through those grueling weeks of workouts and practice.
Now that the day was here, and Joe wasn't, Max
was certain he'd met with foul play. In his words, that
the son-of-a-bitch secretary and that dizzy wife had
finally managed to kill Joe. He made up his mind to
go to the police.

By now the newspapers were calling it a murder,
too. Farnsworth had been missing too long without a
word from any kidnappers, and his business affairs
were not disreputable enough for him to have disappeared. A computer check revealed a Gordian knot
of tangled and interlocking corporate finances, but
that was totally normal for Exo-Grey. So everything
pointed to murder, except that there was no body.

"Lieutenant," said Peters, pushing open the door
to Krim's office, "that trainer Max Corkle is out here.

He says he's got some important information about Farnsworth."

Krim blew out his cheeks in exasperation. "Another son of a bitch wants to get his name in the papers." He sighed. "Tell him to wait." He turned to Conway, frowning. "Anything new on Betty Logan?" he demanded.

Conway shook his head, consulting his notebook. "Nothing. She's led the cleanest life I've ever investigated."

Krim scowled. "A really nice girl, huh?" he snorted. "Then she's got to have murdered him."

Through the glass panes of his office he could see Corkle arguing with Peters, waving his arms and shouting. Suddenly, Corkle broke away from the detective and threw open Krim's door. His face was red and the Rams cap was tilted crazily to one side.

"Corkle, you can't just bust in without knocking," growled Krim.

"Lieutenant, I gotta talk to you!" Corkle was out of breath.

"Even police can't bust in without knocking!" complained Krim. He was a stickler for procedure, and he had the rule book memorized.

"I knew Farnsworth. Nothing in the world could keep him out of that game tonight!"

"And you think that's a good reason to bust in here without knocking?" demanded one-track Krim.

"Forget I busted in! I wanna give you a clue about Farnsworth . . . in private." He looked around significantly at Peters and Conway.

"These guys are my right-hand men," Krim told him huffily. "You can trust them as much as you can trust me."

And how much is that? Corkle asked himself. But he had no choice. Taking a deep breath, he said, "All right, listen." He moved closer to Krim's desk and lowered his voice. "Before Farnsworth disappeared, he told me that his wife and Tony Abbott had tried to kill him. And he told me how. Now you get Abbott down here and let me spring it on him, and I'll make him crack."

Krim scowled, his plump face registering annoyance. After a beat, he said in a grudging tone, "Okay. Wait outside." He watched Peters usher him out.

When the door was shut behind Corkle, Krim glared at it through narrowed eyes. Then he turned resentfully to Conway. "That son of a bitch. He's trying to ruin my case against Betty Logan." Krim hated being sidetracked. Once he'd made up his mind on a suspect, it took a lot of horsepower to pull him off the scent.

There was a knock at the door again, and Peters poked his head around the jamb. "Lieutenant, Mr. Farnsworth's secretary, Mr. Abbott, just called to say Mrs. Farnsworth's leaving for Europe tomorrow night and closing the house."

"What!?" roared Krim, reaching for the phone.

"Wait, I'm not through," Peters went on. "And she's sending the servants to Connecticut to open the house there, and she's taking Abbott with her to handle reservations."

"What?!" yelled Krim again, grabbing at the telephone.

"Wait, I'm almost through. And she called the D.A. and *he* said it was all right."

Krim's hand fell limply from the telephone. This was a lot of horsepower. Standing up, he grabbed his jacket from the back of his chair and struggled into it. "Okay, boys, let's go. We've got to stop her! Conway, you almost went to law school. What can I charge her with?"

Conway thought about it for a few seconds. "Well, you don't have a body and there's no evidence of a crime," he began judiciously. "On the other hand, Mrs. Farnsworth is one of the richest women in the world, and the D.A. said it was all right for her to leave." He shook his head, summing up. "I wouldn't charge her with anything, if I were you."

Krim didn't bother replying. He was thinking of his ace in the old hole, outside, wearing a Rams jacket.

"Pick up Betty Logan and take her out to the Farnsworth house," he barked, throwing his office door open. "You're coming with me," he snapped at Corkle.

"Who, me?" asked Corkle, surprised. "Nah. I gotta be at the Coliseum. The game's in two hours." He started backing off, ready to split.

But Detective Lieutenant Krim had been fired up and was now a man of action. "You just made an accusation of murder. Let's go!"

It was like the last scene in an old Ellery Queen mystery—where Ellery and Inspector Queen line up all the suspects in one room, and they sit around chewing on their nails and displaying their character flaws while Ellery goes on about why this one didn't do it and that one didn't do it, until he comes to the one who did do it, and his accusation is followed by an immediate confession without benefit of lawyer or reading of rights.

Only it wasn't like that scene, because Krim had no idea who did what, and no visible, palpable body for him to see what had been done. He still leaned toward Betty as a suspect, but all those servants! He itched to say a butler did it, just for fun. And Corkle had implicated Mrs. Farnsworth and Abbott. Still, here they all were, spread around the large library of the Farnsworth home, comfortably sitting on sofas and chairs while Krim tried to fit the pieces together.

On one side of the fireplace sat Julia and Tony. Julia had downed two Valium with her brandy, but nothing seemed to work. She was so nervous that only the presence of Tony at her side kept her from jumping up and screaming. Across from them, Betty Logan sat next to Corkle, both of them anxious and unhappy, their minds on Leo Farnsworth.

Most of the staff had been rounded up, too, and were sitting as quietly and unobtrusively as they could, all the while hating police procedure. Krim had sent for Everett, Bentley, Sisk, Corinne, and Lavinia, and, of course, the chauffeur and the chief security guard. All of them wore the noncommittal faces that make servants practically invisible. On the other hand, Corkle was very obviously nervous. That was because the Super Bowl was starting in ten minutes, and he was a long, long way from the Coliseum, and try to explain *that* to Figarello and Judson!

Peters and Conway dutifully scribbled notes while Krim tried to create order out of this complicated bowl of macaroni. He was working on the servants now.

"Well, let me get this all straight," he said to Sisk. "Are you trying to tell me you saw no specific change in Mr. Farnsworth's behavior?"

Sisk thought for a moment. "Nooo," he said at last. "I did notice that he seemed to take a dislike to his hats, but it was never violent."

Corkle was too antsy now to sit through any more talk of hats. What about Abbott and Julia? He jumped up from his chair. "Look, why don't you ask me whatever it is and let me get to the Coliseum?"

"Mr. Corkle, please!" Lieutenant Krim's answer was sharp. He conducted an investigation very methodically, in his own way, and he hated interruptions. Now he turned to Everett.

"Mr. Everett. You had cocoa with him every night at nine. What did you and he talk about? Just give me a general example."

"Well, he would say something like 'This carob cocoa is good,' and I would answer, 'Yes, it is,' although frankly, I prefer ordinary cocoa, and then he'd say something like 'I wish the marshmallow lasted a little bit longer,' and I would say something like 'So do I,' and occasionally we would talk about whole-grain cookies. . . ."

"Nothing about hats?" demanded Krim.

"Never, sir."

Corkle sat back down, his shoulders bowing in defeat.

He'd never make it to the Super Bowl now. He saw a color television set in the corner of the library. The game would be on soon. If he could at least watch it on TV . . . his fingers made knob-twisting motions without his being aware of them.

Meanwhile, out in the garden, the Japanese gardener had finished with the lawns and the flower beds. It was time to get on to emptying the fountains of dead leaves, and cleaning up the wishing well. He decided to start first on the well, because he was particularly short of cash right now, and the bucket in the well usually yielded up eight to ten dollars in coins. But the rope wouldn't pull. He peered down into the well. It was too dark and too deep to see anything. He tugged on the rope again. Funny, he thought, the rope is stuck. He tugged on it harder, and with more enthusiasm. Maybe the bucket was so full of money that it was too heavy to rise. Good thought! Wrapping the free end of the rope around his waist and digging in his heels, the gardener pulled harder and harder.

"Mr. Abbott." Krim turned his attention now to the executive secretary, who sat, coolly attired in a nautical blazer and ascot, on the sofa beside Mrs. Farnsworth. "What did you and Mr. Farnsworth talk about the last time you saw him?"

"He was considering buying Haiti," Abbott responded smoothly.

"The country?" croaked Krim incredulously.

"Yes, sir."

Joe and Mr. Jordan came into the library, invisible, and stood watching the investigation proceed. Joe's eyes were fixed on Betty.

"Thank you, Mr. Abbott. Nothing about hats?"

"No, sir."

"Thank you very much." Krim turned to Julia Farnsworth, who was sitting on the sofa willing to give her left foot for the chance to bite off a nail. "Now,

Mrs. Farnsworth. What was the relationship between you and your husband?"

"Very, very special," answered Julia immediately. "Very, very close." Out of the corner of her eye she could see Betty Logan looking surprised. Serves her right, the little bitch.

"Did you know," continued Krim, pacing, "that Miss Logan claims your husband told her that he was getting a divorce, and asked her to—"

"Marry him?" Julia interrupted. "I don't doubt that, Lieutenant. You see, although my husband loved me very, very much"—and here she managed to inject just the hint of a sob into her voice—" he was a man who would do or say anything to make a conquest."

Joe opened his mouth to protest, but shut it again when he realized that what Julia was saying was probably true . . . of Farnsworth. Besides, nobody could see or hear him, anyway.

"But that never touched our marriage." Julia tried on a brave little smile to see if it would fit. "That's what made it so very, very special. That's why we were so very, very close. I'm sorry, Miss Logan, if I've said anything to hurt you." Julia smiled, lying through her teeth.

"That's all right," said Betty evenly. "I don't know you well enough for you to hurt me."

"I *hope* you don't doubt my word," Julia purred.

"I don't," retorted Betty calmly. "I'm absolutely certain that you're lying."

"They're trying to pin it on Betty," said Joe to Mr. Jordan, concern showing on his face.

"You needn't worry about her, Joe."

But Joe was anxious. Now that he saw her again, he could see that she looked exhausted and unhappy. Her large eyes were shadowed by worry, and her full lips were drawn tightly together. More than anything in the world, Joe wanted to gather her up in his arms and kiss her worried look away. But he didn't even have the arms to hold her with.

"I assume, Miss Logan," Krim was saying, "that if Mr. Farnsworth had told you he disliked his hats, you would let us know."

This was too much for Max Corkle. He leaped up from his seat. "Look, you wanna know about hats?" he shouted. "I'll tell you, once and for all. He didn't mind wearing hats. But he wouldn't wear socks with a suit!"

Lieutenant Krim looked startled. No socks! Here was a new line of investigation.

"He'd put on a pinstripe," Max went on, "and black oxfords, and when he crossed his legs, you could see that his ankles were bare. *That's* why he stopped wearing hats. He thought they looked funny without socks."

"I see," mused Krim, carefully mulling over this new bit of evidence. "But he never actually told you he disliked them?"

"What?"

"His hats!"

Corkle saw stars. And they thought *Joe* was crazy! Football players were the nuttiest bunch of guys Corkle had ever encountered as a group. But that was before he'd met up with cops. "Listen!" he roared. "Are you crazy? What kind of investigation is this? Hats! Socks! Meanwhile, I'm missing the Super Bowl!" He made a dive for the TV set, but Peters and Conway stopped him before he could switch it on.

"All right, all right, *all right!*" yelled Krim. "Turn that thing on. Let him watch his football game."

Peters and Conway jumped to the task. They'd been dying to have a look at the game, too. They settled themselves before the screen, one on either side of Corkle. The game had already begun.

Betty sat alone, her eyes cast down, misery written all over her beautiful features. Joe went to her, knelt at her side, looked intently into her eyes. His own were filled with love and longing, but she couldn't see him.

"Betty, listen to me, Betty," Joe whispered urgently. "Don't worry. Everything's gonna be all right. I promise you, Betty. I love you." He knew she couldn't hear him, and it was cutting him up badly.

Betty stirred a little, suddenly uneasy. A vivid memory of a pair of deep blue eyes had blotted out everything in the room, leaving her lonelier and more miserable than ever.

"All right, Mr. Abbott, what you're telling me is that Mr. Farnsworth never carried any money or credit cards with him, right?" Still pacing, Krim's eyes drifted to the TV screen, where the Steelers had just thrown a thirty-five-yard completion. The ball was on the Rams' eight-yard line, first and goal for the Steelers.

"Right." Abbott nodded briskly.

"And . . . no—" Krim broke off, his eyes returning to the game. The Rams had just given up a touchdown pass to Pittsburgh. Corkle groaned, his hands clutching at his thinning hair, his face contorted.

"And no identification papers. Right?" asked Krim, tearing his eyes away from the screen.

"None," agreed Abbott promptly. "Right, sir."

"So then what we have here is a man who suddenly starts liking football . . . and . . . at the same time . . . stops wearing socks and hats, and who . . . disappears . . . with no . . . credit cards . . ." concluded Krim lamely, his eyes frankly glued now to the television screen.

Everybody in the room was openly watching the game now, even Julia and the maids. Betty, as she looked at the TV set, kept recalling how *he* was supposed to be playing today, how much *he* had wanted to. And now the team was losing, too.

A disaster. Corkle was writhing like a madman, chomping on his cigar butt, muttering curses at the opposing players, groaning and whimpering. Joe, standing behind the wing chair in which Betty sat, was torn between looking at her and looking at the game. The Rams were trying a play that Joe was familiar with, but it required split-second timing and Jarrett appeared to be off. When the ball was snapped, he dropped back

145

into the pocket instead of rolling out to his right. There was no way to avoid two blitzing Steeler linebackers and Jarrett was smeared from his blind side just as he was about to throw the ball. As the other players got up, Jarrett lay motionless on the field.   ..

"He's hurt. Tom Jarrett's hurt and it looks serious," yelled the announcer into his microphone, while the more than seventy thousand fans in the stands stood up and craned their necks for a better look. From the Rams' benches a flurry of activity and Figarello and Judson ran out onto the field.

In the Farnsworth library, everybody crowded around the TV set for a better view. Corkle's fists were tightly clenched, his face a tormented white mask.

"Oh, oh," muttered Peters. "Looks like Jarrett is really hurt."

"What happened?" demanded Krim, pushing his way to the front. "It's Jarrett. Jesus, they really sacked him. Look, he's out cold." A gurney was being wheeled onto the turf at a run, and two team doctors were kneeling at Jarrett's side.

Mr. Jordan moved quietly to the television set and stood in front of it, invisible to everybody but Joe. He beckoned to Joe, as if to say, "It's time now," and Joe, suddenly, painfully, began to understand.

Meanwhile, down at the wishing well, the small gardener, with utter patience, had managed to get the rope pulled up far enough to tie it to a tree. Only a few more feet to go. Buddha, it was heavy! Treasure, perhaps? If the prize was rich enough, he could quit this job and go into the plastic bonsai business. With an incredible burst of effort for so small a man, he gave the rope one final tug. The whatever-it-was rose slowly, slowly to the surface of the well. When it was close enough to be seen, the gardener took a good, long look. Then, shrieking, he let the rope drop and the whole thing plummeted back to the bottom again.

"Mrs. Farnsworth, the Haitian Ambassador is here," said Sisk, coming in with a card on a silver tray.

Julia looked a little blank, but Tony jabbed her silently in the ribs. "Oh!" cried Julia. "Oh, yes . . . yes, thank you, Sisk."

"Give him a Coke and tell him to wait," ordered Krim.

This was too much for Julia's frayed nerve endings. "Who do you think you are?" she shrieked suddenly at the police lieutenant. "This is my home. What is this, an interrogation or a social club?" Almost hysterically, she waved a hand at the group of people, strangers, who were crowded around her television set. "I've never seen anything conducted like this in my life!" Her voice rose from a shrill squeak to a near scream.

This was the moment that Krim had been waiting for, when Julia Farnsworth's emotional defense mechanism had ceased to function.

"Now! Corkle now!" He said, signaling him urgently with his eyes.

Corkle tore himself away from the television set, his head still in the Coliseum with his losing team. "Huh?" he said blankly.

"*NOW*!" insisted Krim, jerking his head at Julia.

But Corkle was slow to comprehend. "Now what?" he asked fuzzily, then the light dawned. "Oh, yeah." He took a few steps forward, confronting Julia Farnsworth directly. "How did you do it *this* time?" he demanded.

"What?" squealed Julia, taken completely by surprise.

"Did you drug him and stick him in the bathtub again, like you did before?"

"What are you talking about?" Julia started to get up, but Tony Abbott grabbed her and pulled her down again, clamping his hand over her mouth. At the feel and smell of that familiar palm, something snapped in Julia Farnsworth, and her muffled hysteria began to curl around the edges of Abbott's strong hand and come out into the open.

Jarrett was still unconscious. He hadn't moved a muscle, hadn't even moaned since the moment he'd been faced by the Steelers' linebackers. His face was an unearthly white, and his breathing and pulse were shallow and slow and becoming shallower and slower every second.

One of the doctors shook his head and looked over at Figarello and Judson. "From the look of the pupils," he said gravely, "it's probably a fracture or an aneurysm that ruptured when he got hit."

"Jesus," said Judson softly, and Figarello swallowed wordlessly. Only twenty-seven years old. And not even into his prime. First Pendleton, now Jarrett. Was there a curse on the Los Angeles Rams?

Mr. Jordan looked at Joe. "Make up your mind, Joe. You have only a few seconds."

But Joe was staring down at Jarrett, agonized. Tears were forming in his eyes. "Oh, God!" he yelled at Mr. Jordan. "What did you do, kill him, too?"

Mr. Jordan shook his head. "Thomas Jarrett was always slated to die at this moment, Joe. Now listen to me. You have a chance to fulfill your destiny."

"What kinda destiny is it to turn into Jarrett?" Joe demanded hotly.

"He was a great football player. And so are you. You can be unbeatable now. It's your destiny."

But Joe still hesitated. Football was no longer the first thing on his mind. "I don't care about any destiny," he burst out. "All I care about is Betty. Don't you understand?"

But Mr. Jordan's expression did not change. He looked at Joe with an almost melancholy solemnity. "This was our agreement. You will have the body you deserve."

"She's the only thing I care about," murmured Joe. Even *he* was surprised to learn how true this was. It was nothing he'd ever experienced before. It had never been in his original game plan, to fall in love.

"You have three seconds, Joe," said Mr. Jordan hypnotically. "Jarrett's a great football player, and you know it. The truth is, you'd even like to be like him." His face was oddly lit by a radiance that Joe had never seen before; he could hardly take his eyes off Mr. Jordan. Something strange was happening to him. He felt suddenly very weird, as if he were melting. Something was definitely happening.

CHAPTER XII

The transition was immediate. Joe felt the gurney rolling along the sidelines. It jostled him into consciousness. But he couldn't see a thing. Then he realized that his eyes were closed. Slowly he opened them.

Several anxious faces were bent in a circle over him. It took several seconds before they realized that he was staring back at them. The disbelief that was playing over their faces was proof enough to Joe that once again he was living in someone else's body.

The cameras zoomed in on the sidelines, where Tom Jarrett had risen from the gurney and was jogging in place, as though testing his limbs. A roar filled the stadium as he ran out into the field. Jarrett was all right! He was coming back into the game!

"Hey, look!" yelled Conway, pointing to the screen.

"It's Jarrett!" Peters was flushed with excitement, his plain face lit up by a wide grin. "Jarrett's back in the game!"

Tony and Julia stopped squabbling to look, and Corkle, disbelieving, roughly pushed Peters aside to get a better look at the screen.

"It's like a miracle," Krim breathed. "I thought he was dead."

A miracle, yeah, thought Max. It had to be. Look at him go, better than ever. Better than Jarrett. As good as Pendleton—Joe! It had to be.

Of all the people in the room, only Betty Logan sat uncaring. How could they all get so excited about a game, when nobody had found out yet what had happened to *him?* The investigation, the accusations that Max Corkle had been making against Julia Farnsworth, all were forgotten only because a football player proved to be uninjured. Betty sank lower into her chair, her small fists pressed against her temples. Deep inside her, she had felt that he was dead, but had pushed that belief away from her conscious mind. But Max Corkle's accusations had had the ring of truth to them. He was dead. If he weren't, he'd be playing in the Super Bowl, and she'd be there, cheering him on. It was true, then. He wasn't ever coming back.

A sudden commotion outside the library roused Betty from her sad musings and took the others' attention away from the TV. The gardener, shouting in Japanese, ran in without knocking, carrying a man's jacket, dripping wet. In the back was a large bullet hole.

"Oh, my God!" screamed Julia before she could stop herself. "That's his jacket!" Recognizing her mistake instantly, she dissolved into fragments. "It's all your fault!" she shrieked at Tony Abbott. "I told you you'd screw it up! You did it!"

Krim turned coolly to his assistant. "All right, Peters. Book them."

By the time Peters had shot across the long room and grabbed Tony by the blazer, he and Julia were in a screaming match, trading accusations like baseball cards. It looked as though the case had been solved, just like in the Ellery Queen mysteries.

Max Corkle straightened his Rams cap and headed for the door.

"Corkle! Where do you think you're going?!" Krim yelled after him.

"I'm going to the Coliseum," replied Max without breaking stride.

"Wait, Corkle!" barked the lieutenant. "I'm conducting an investigation here!"

At the door, Max turned and faced the others. "Now,

look. I'm going to the game. If you want me to stay, arrest me. Otherwise, take this investigation and stuff it!" And he was gone.

The Rams were suddenly on fire. On the Steelers' twenty-nine yard line, Joe was backpedaling, pumping his arm trying to find a receiver.

In seven quick plays, Joe had led the team forty-five yards down the field. It was now fourth down and three to go. The head coach had tried to send in the field goal unit but Joe had waved them off.

The gamble was not a Jarrett-like move, but Joe didn't care. It was his game now to win or lose. He was calling the shots.

Joe caught sight of Cassidy, his fleet-footed wide receiver, streaking down the sideline and faking once to the middle he released the ball.

Cassidy had to lunge flat out but at the last moment his huge hands closed around the ball like a vise. He landed just inside the end zone. The Rams fans went wild. Their team had suddenly come alive.

The extra point attempt was good and the score board flashed—Steelers 28–Rams 24.

While the fired-up defensive team valiantly tried to contain the powerful Steeler offense, Joe was behind the bench throwing pass after pass. The hysteria of the Rams fans rained down all around him, but Joe was totally absorbed in trying to get used to his new body. Jarrett's body was taller and leaner and Joe was racing against the clock trying to coordinate his passing action with his new arms. Again and again he threw the ball correcting his rhythm and perfecting his ball release to take advantage of every new potential.

Too keyed up at suddenly finding himself in the middle of the Super Bowl Joe couldn't pause long enough to assess any of his feelings. But he was vaguely aware of a growing sense of ease and well-being. And, he was gratefully thanking Tom Jarrett for being such a dedicated athlete.

Max Corkle kept his eyes glued to the road, but all his attention was focused on the car radio. With every play the sportscaster described, every point the Rams scored, every yard of ground they gained, Max was more and more convinced that Joe Pendleton was playing the Super Bowl. Jarrett had been good, damn good. But the moves he was hearing about on the radio had Pendleton written all over them.

Chuckling gleefully, Max put on a burst of speed as he neared the Coliseum. He was going to see *some* game, if there was any of it left by the time he got there. A combination of Joe Pendleton's brain and Tom Jarrett's body—unbeatable. All Joe had needed was legs that would hold out, and now he had them. Joe Pendleton in a twenty-seven-year-old body, with a reach as long as the San Andreas fault. Corkle could hardly wait.

But that wasn't all. Max wanted to see *Joe* again. That was the main thing. It had been wonderful in those last few weeks before Farnsworth had disappeared, working with Joe, talking with him, even listening to him play that old saxophone of his. He missed the man more than he missed the football player, and he could hardly wait to see his friend again, even though it would be weird to look into Jarrett's face. Especially if it had Joe's eyes. Except . . . didn't Jarrett and Joe have the same color eyes to begin with?

Max's thoughts turned to Betty. Now there was a nice girl. Not only beautiful and smart, but filled with a warmth that made you happy just to know her. Poor kid, she was all broken up about Joe. Even if she never knew him as Joe. Was there a chance that maybe she and Jarrett could get together? After all, it was still Joe, right? Who was gonna tell her he was alive? Not me. Don't look at me. And not Mr. Jordan. He never said a word you could hear. So that left Joe, and Corkle didn't envy him. Not everybody had the instinctual trust of a Max Corkle; she'd probably think that the tall young quarterback was nuts. On the other hand, she was in love with Joe, and if Max Corkle could be convinced immediately that Joe was Farnsworth, then maybe this girl could tell, too. Anyway, he'd be on hand to help his old pal out.

There were only a few minutes left to play. Max was going to miss the Super Bowl. A flood of regret washed over him, but then he remembered that he had some news that would interest Joe. Mrs. Farnsworth and Abbott had finally been nailed and he, Corkle, had had a hand in it. Joe would be proud of him.

The Steelers were marching relentlessly down the field grinding out three and four yards at a time. Time was running out. Max turned off at the Coliseum exit and down the freeway ramp. Cars were everywhere. There wasn't a parking space within three miles. He sat alone, trapped in the front seat of his car, listening to the climax of the Super Bowl game. Only about a minute of play left. Suddenly, the impossible happened. Pittsburgh fumbled and the Rams recovered on their own twenty-two.

As Joe ran back out onto the field, he glanced up at the scoreboard clock. One minute and sixteen seconds remained. This was it. There would be no second chances.

Joe stepped into the huddle feeling fresh and full of reserve power. A series of plays had been sent in from the bench. Joe put them aside, firmly silencing several of his startled teammates, and called a new series. He knew that the Steelers would be in a prevent-defensive and that only daring, imaginative plays were going to work.

Breaking the huddle he stepped up behind his center studying the defense, probing for weaknesses.

After barking out several audibles, he took the snap, dropped back, faking a draw into the line, and threw. The ball soared over the heads of the stunting linebackers and was snatched in the flats by Owens, his big tight end.

A nineteen yard gain.

Another first down.

Again, a play came in from the bench and again Joe overruled it. He threw a quick down and out to Cassidy who grabbed the ball just before he stepped out of bounds, stopping the clock with forty-eight seconds left. First and ten on the Steeler forty-five.

Time was running out. In the huddle, Joe called three plays in order to save time. They had to work.

He took the snap and dropped back into the pocket looking for Cassidy on the sideline. But, he was too well covered and Joe had to go to a secondary receiver who was hit hard before he could get out of bounds.

The clock ticked mercilessly on—33 . . . 32 . . . 31 . . . 30 as his teammates tried to get set. No more time outs. No stopping the clock—25 . . . 24 . . . 23 . . . 22. Joe took the ball and started to roll-out to the right but the pressure from the defense was too great and Joe was forced to scramble. Desperately he looked down field as he neatly eluded a big Steeler defensive end but again all his receivers were well covered. Out of the corner of his eye he spotted Evans, the fullback, open about eight yards down in the flat and he rifled the ball. Evans caught the ball and seeing that he was about to be tackled, started to reverse his field.

Just as he did so, one of the Steeler defensive backs lunged at him sending him crashing to the turf. The ball squirted loose and bounced crazily across the field. Joe who, when Evans had made his move, had raced over to try to block for him, stuck out his hands and grabbed the ball.

Everywhere he looked he saw black and gold Steeler jerseys and the goal line seemed miles away, but Joe ran like a man possessed. Following what little blocking there was, he sped down the field, wheeling, turning, feinting, spinning off tackles until only one Steeler defender was between him and the end zone.

As the defensive back lined up his man on the five yard line, Joe launched himself into the air, sailed by the stunned Pittsburgh back and landed just over the goal line.

He'd done it! Joe Pendleton had carried the ball forty-five yards for a TD, right through the strongest defense in the National Football League. Max could hear the crowd chanting Jarrett's name as the final score went up on the board—Rams 30, Steelers 28.

Max switched off the radio and got out of the car quickly. He wanted to see Joe for himself, see him and give him a hug and tell him he'd be on his side no matter whose body he was in. He ran to the side door of the stadium, pushing open the employees' entrance door, and made his way to the gate.

The jubilant Rams had lifted Jarrett to their shoulders and carried him off the field to the locker room. Waiting at the gate was a crowd of fans, and Max started to push his way through them. At first, nobody would let him go by, but when they spotted his Rams jacket and cap, they acknowledged his right to pass and they made way for him. Max ran down the ramp toward the tunnel leading to the locker room.

Inside the locker room, everything was noise, light, confusion, and jubilation, with football players pouring Mumm's Extra Dry champagne over one another's heads. The TV crews were on hand, and some of the top names in sportscasting and writing were clustered around Tom Jarrett, the wonder who'd pulled the Rams back from the brink of defeat and carried them to victory almost singlehandedly. The sound of congratulations and laughter nearly deafened Max as he got to the locker-room door. The place was jammed, and standing in the center of the jam was a grinning Tom Jarrett, the focus of everybody's attention.

Corkle fought his way through the crush of players and reporters, finally managing to get Joe's attention. They embraced warmly, slapping each other heartily on the back as Corkle bellowed, "It's really you, isn't it Joe? Boy, they sure bump 'em off up there don't they."

Joe grinned from ear to ear and hugged Corkle again.

Now a TV reporter followed by a mini-cam came homing in on the young quarterback.

"Well, Tom Jarrett, the star of the Super Bowl, this is the moment your whole life has been coming to, right?"

Squinting a little in the lights, Joe smiled broadly. "Yeah . . . right . . . the moment my whole life has been coming to . . . right."

"Could you describe it for us?"

As Joe opened his mouth to speak, he saw Mr. Jordan standing behind the TV reporter, watching him with pride and compassion. "I . . . uh . . . well . . . I . . ." began Joe.

"I've got to go now, Joe," said Mr. Jordan. "It's time. I can't stay any longer." His words had a ring of finality that confused and frightened Joe.

"What do you mean?" he asked, his eyes fixed on Mr. Jordan.

"I mean, tell us what it's like at this moment to be Tom Jarrett," the newsman persisted.

"And when I'm gone," said Mr. Jordan, "you won't remember me. You'll be Thomas Jarrett, with no memory of Joe Pendleton . . . or Leo Farnsworth . . . or anything that happened."

"Wait! Wait! What about Betty?" Joe called out.

That sacking must have hit Jarrett hard in the head, thought the newsman. He wasn't making any sense.

"It's all right, Joe." Mr. Jordan's voice, quiet as it was, cut like magic through the pandemonium in the locker room. "You won't remember. You have a new life now."

Panic contorted Joe's features. "What do you mean I won't remember?" he demanded, agonized. "I *have* to remember! You gotta wait!"

"There's a design in everything. This is your destiny, Joe. You're back on your own road. Goodbye." He was starting to fade. Joe could hardly see him any more, and his voice was thin, almost without timbre or tone.

The TV reporter was trying to salvage the interview, even though it was obvious to him that Jarrett needed a long rest in a quiet place. While the camera was rolling, he was paid to keep things moving, and he said to Jarrett now, "Perhaps if we showed you a replay, you'd remember. I know you have a lot of things going through your mind—"

"No, wait! Wait! I gotta talk to you, Mr. Jordan! Don't go! Please, Mr. Jordan. I gotta talk to you!"

Who the hell was Mr. Jordan? the sportscaster wondered. Max Corkle could have told him, but Max was clear across the locker room. It was time to get the camera off Jarrett, before the football fans of the world formed the wrong opinion of the boy's mental abilities. Signaling to the cameraman, the TV reporter moved on to one of the other players.

"Goodbye, Joe. Goodbye." The voice was indistinct, almost disembodied. It was a wisp of eternity, caught in the now for the briefest instant. Then it was gone. Tom Jarrett shook his head to clear it. All this goddamn noise was getting to him.

Judson was ushering the doctor through the crowd, bringing him over to where Jarrett stood looking hopelessly at thin air. "Tom, let's talk for a minute. You took a pretty nasty hit on the head." Judson took the boy by the elbow and moved him to one side, where he and the doctor could talk to him privately. Jarrett was looking kind of dazed, he thought, and he didn't like that look in his eyes, especially where the swelling was turning dark purple. The doctor held the crowd back for him, and Tom and the head coach moved through it quietly until they reached the trainers' room, which was empty and quiet.

"Tom," said Judson with concern. "Are you all right?"

"Yeah." Tom's head was really aching now.

"What is it you were trying to remember?" the head coach asked curiously.

"I don't know," said Tom blankly.

"Sit down, kid. Sit down." The coach prodded Jarrett gently, and the boy took a seat on one of the treatment tables. "Tom, you know where you are?" he asked gently.

Jarrett looked around him and gave a short laugh. "Do I know where I am? C'mon, Coach," he scoffed.

"What's your name?" persisted the coach.

Jarrett grinned. "Some people call me Tom, but you can call me Sixteen," he kidded, pointing to the number on his jersey.

The coach whistled in relief, just as the doctor pushed his way into the room and closed the door behind him.

"For a minute you had me a little scared there," admitted Judson. "I want you to lie down for a while and let Doc take a long look at you."

Jarrett *was* feeling punk; he hoisted his long, muscular legs up on the vinyl-covered table and stretched out, shutting his eyes and enjoying the stink of liniment and disinfectant and athletic gear that the trainers' room always smelled of. He winced a little as the doctor's trained fingers probed the area around his puffy eye, but he relaxed. It was all over now, and he was in good hands. Besides, wasn't he a hero? He smiled to himself.

Betty drove anxiously toward the Coliseum. She hated driving on the wrong side of the road; it made her nervous. But she felt she must see Max Corkle, must find him and talk to him about . . . she couldn't even say it to herself. But Corkle had been his only friend, besides herself. The only one who cared for him for his own sake and not for the money or the power. She needed Max now. She needed his strength and his practicality and his rough kindliness. Desperately, she needed a shoulder to cry on, somebody who would understand, who'd known the man she loved.

The locker room was almost empty now. Corkle thought that maybe it was the right time, maybe he'd get a chance to talk to Joe alone now. The players had packed up their gear and left, a bunch of happy men, thousands of dollars of victors' money richer, and the TV crews and the yelling fans had long since departed. Joe hadn't come out yet; Max knew that he was lying down inside somewhere, resting from his long evening and the bruising aftermath of the game. The only man left in the locker room was the doctor, who was neatly repacking his bag with his medical equipment.

"Joe," called Corkle, then catching himself. "Uh, Tom? Tom? Hey, Doc, did Tom leave yet?"

The doctor snapped his black leather case shut. "Nope. He's just putting some ice on his eye. He'll be out in a minute." He picked up his hat and headed for the door, then stopped and looked at Max curiously. "Hey, that's something about Farnsworth, huh?" he said. They all knew that Corkle had been training with Farnsworth on his own time. "Poor son of a bitch, terrible thing to happen."

"Yeah," said Max absently. "Terrible."

"Well, good night, Max."

"Good night, Doc."

He was alone. He stood up, suddenly bone-weary. The events of the evening were beginning to catch up with him; he oughta be home in bed by now, a guy his age. But he wanted, he needed, to see Joe. He was the only man on earth who knew what had happened; and he wanted to give Joe one great big hug and a "welcome back." Pendleton had saved the day. He wanted to tell him about Julia and that dimwit Abbott, too.

He turned to go into the trainers' room, where he he surmised Joe would be resting, when he caught sight of something. That something made Max Corkle grin broadly. It was a saxophone, a soprano saxophone—Joe's old sax.

"Well, hello there," said Max to the sax. "I was expecting to see you around here somewhere. I never thought the day would come when I'd be glad to see *you*."

"Hey, Corkle, what are you doing here? Closing up the joint? Talking to yourself?"

Max looked up, startled. Tom Jarrett, stripped to the waist, an ice bag pressed against his swelling eye, walked into the locker room and headed for the locker marked "16." Flipping open the door, he threw the ice bag onto a shelf and reached for his shirt.

Max just stood and watched him, wary and puzzled. He wasn't sure what to say. Jarrett's . . . Joe's . . . lack of intimacy disturbed him and put him on his guard.

"Hey, I didn't know you played that thing," said Jarrett, pointing to the saxophone in Corkle's hand.

"What are you talking about?" Max moved a little closer to Jarrett, trying to look into his eyes, but as the young man dressed, he kept the swollen side of his face turned to Max.

"Is that yours?" asked Jarrett, making conversation.

"What are you talking about?" Corkle asked again, unable to believe his ears. This was Joe, at least it *had been* Joe.

"What do you mean, what am I talking about?" Jarrett stepped into his slacks and zipped up the fly.

"I mean, what are you talking about?" repeated Corkle. He held the sax out at arm's length toward Jarrett, so that Joe would see that Max didn't want to be kidded any more. He needed reassurance; it had been a very long day.

"Did I miss something?" asked Jarrett vaguely sarcastic.

"Hey, come on, what are you trying to do to me?" With a trembling hand, Max poured himself a glass of flat champagne and tossed it back with a single swallow.

"Hey, I'm the guy who got hit on the head, not you," laughed Jarrett. "Are you all right, Corkle?" He glanced at himself in the small locker mirror and reached in to get his jacket.

"Come on, play something for me," urged Corkle, holding the saxophone out and coming closer to Jarrett.

Jarrett was slipping into his jacket, straightening the lapels. "That's what happens when you drink champagne." He grinned. "You just keep pouring it down because it doesn't taste like anything . . . then, all of a sudden, you're drunk." He gave a bemused little shake of his head that drove Corkle up the wall. "You going to the party, Corkle? I'll give you a ride."

Suddenly, Max realized that this man wasn't kidding. Something had happened, he was certain of it. Something had recently taken away Joe's memory. Because he was certain it had been Joe, thinking on his feet like that, pulling the team up from behind, winning. Jarrett couldn't have done it by himself. Somewhere in there was Joe Pendleton, and he'd admitted as much to Corkle. Max couldn't figure why he wasn't coming out.

"You're not trying to tell me you don't remember me, do you?" asked Max quietly.

Tom Jarrett laughed. "I remember you fine, and I think a little fresh air wouldn't hurt."

"Do me a favor, will you?" Corkle pleaded. "Look at me. Come on. Look straight at me."

Jarrett turned, mystified, but he did as Corkle asked. He looked straight at him, for a long moment. Max's eyes probed the other's deeply. It was so hard to tell. They had the same color eyes, Joe and Tom, and one of them was all swollen and bruised. Yet, was there something . . . some glint that was familiar? He

163

thought he could see something . . . yes . . . no . . .
now it was gone. It was definitely gone. And it probably had never been there. Max Corkle was looking
at Tom Jarrett, star quarterback of the Los Angeles
Rams. He'd lost Joe Pendleton for good.

"Joe . . . Joe . . ." he said heartbrokenly, sinking
onto a bench.

"Ah, you wanna tell me why you're calling me Joe?"
asked Tom with a slight edge in his voice.

"I . . . I guess it has something to do with Joe
Pendleton," said Corkle with a frog in his throat.

A moment of silence fell while both men thought of
Pendleton. Jarrett realized that Max had had one too
many, but he now understood why. Corkle had been
very close to Pendleton, and this might have been
Pendleton's night, not his.

"I'm sorry, Max" said Jarrett gently, sitting on the
bench and putting his arm around Corkle's shoulder.
"I wasn't thinking." He remembered the sax. Didn't
Pendleton play the saxophone? Sure, they all used to
kid him about it.

He clapped Max on the shoulder. "Well, we won,"
he said more cheerfully. "You sure you don't want a
ride?"

Max shook his head, unable to speak. A sense of
great loneliness and sadness gripped him. "No, I think
I'll just sit here for a while," he said finally.

"Okay." Jarrett stood up and headed for the locker
room door. "See you."

"You played a hell of a game, Tom," Max called
after him.

"Thanks, Corkle. You're sure you're all right?"

"Yeah." Max nodded.

"Okay. See you later. I'm just gonna slip out this
way." He left the locker room, closing the door quietly
behind him.

Corkle sat silently, hunched on the bench, grieving.
He was alone, very alone. Unconsciously, his hand
grasped the saxophone and he pressed a few of its

keys. No sound came out. He couldn't play it, either. Probably nobody would ever play it again. But he'd take it home with him, just in case. You never knew.

Betty had had a difficult time persuading the custodian that she was a friend of Max Corkle's and that she had to see him. But he had given in at last, won over by her sincerity, and opened the gates for her. Now she was walking swiftly down the corridor leading to the locker rooms, looking for Max. She needed to be with him now because she couldn't trust herself to be alone.

She saw a tall young man coming down the corridor, strapping on his wristwatch.

"Excuse me," she said quietly. The young man stopped. "I wonder if you could tell me where I could find a Mr. Max Corkle. I believe he's along here somewhere."

English. She's English, Jarrett noted automatically, but his mind was elsewhere. "Yeah," he said politely. "He's in the locker room. You can go back out the way you came in, or you can go down there"—he pointed to the opposite end of the corridor—"and take a right, then a left, and it's the second doorway on the right."

"I see. Thank you," said Betty quietly.

She's pretty, but her face is so sad, thought Jarrett. What's a pretty girl like her got to be so sad about? He turned to watch her walk away, when suddenly she turned, too, and looked back at him.

"He's . . . he's not expecting me," she said hesitantly. "Do you think it's all right just to walk straight in?"

She looked up at him, her head tilted to one side.

"Sure," he said, moving toward her without thinking twice. There was a magnetism about her that attracted him . . . he followed her like a pile of iron filings. "He's the only person in there. Go right in." He couldn't take his eyes off her. Her eyes were the largest, most beautiful, deepest eyes he'd ever seen.

What color were they? And, there was something vaguely familiar about her.

Betty stopped, looking at him carefully. There was something . . . arresting about him . . . something that made her stare back. He was very good-looking, but that wasn't it. There was something more, something underneath . . .

"Have we met?" he asked her softly.

"No, I don't think so," she replied slowly.

Jarrett shook his head. "No, I guess not. But for a minute there, I was sure I knew you." He nodded and was about to turn and walk away, but he was strangely reluctant to leave her. "What did you think of the game?" he asked with a shy smile.

"I didn't see it," Betty confessed.

He felt a pang of disappointment. He wanted her to have seen it and to know who he was. Kid stuff. "Oh. Well, we won."

"Did you? Congratulations" Betty smiled at him and the smile washed his disappointment away.

"Thanks." He knew that he should go, but he couldn't seem to get his feet to move. He just wanted to stand there and look at her. She had the softest hair he'd ever seen, thick and light and curly.

Betty looked up at his face. His brow and cheekbone were very badly bruised, and one of his eyes was puffy and swollen. "Your eye is hurt," she said, concerned.

Jarrett touched the bruise on his face as if feeling it for the first time. He shook his head. Then he held his hand out to her. "My name is Tom Jarrett," he said.

Her hand was very soft, but her handshake was firm. "I'm Betty Logan," she said. "Hello."

"Nice to meet you," said Jarrett, forcing himself to let go of her hand.

"Do you play for the Rams," said Betty.

"Yeah. You interested in football?" he asked her hopefully. She hadn't even recognized his name.

"Well, no. But a friend of mine was."

"Was?"

"Leo Farnsworth," the girl said simply.

"I'm sorry," said Jarrett huskily. "Was he a close friend?"

The girl's face darkened as a shadow fell across it. "Yes. Very close."

"That's too bad. I'm sorry," he said again.

He looks so sympathetic. He has such a warm expression in his eyes . . . well, eye, Betty corrected herself. Then she did something she found very odd, but she couldn't stop herself. Without even thinking about it, she reached up and pushed the tumbling dark hair away from the bruise on his forehead. I've touched a stranger, she thought. How unlike me. But it's his eyes. There's something about them . . . Aloud she said, "You should put some ice on that. It looks nasty."

"Yeah," said Tom.

Suddenly, the lights went off.

"What's that?" asked Betty, alarmed.

"Don't be scared," Tom reassured her. "They're just closing up the place. Just stay close to me. There's nothing to be afraid of." He reached his hand out into the darkness and took hers. "I know where we're going."

He led her to a door in the corridor wall and opened it, revealing an exit. Now they were in the corridor that led to the stadium and the outside world.

"What did you say?" Betty asked him, moving close to look up into his face.

"What?" said Tom, surprised.

"Just then. You said, 'There's nothing to be afraid of.' Your voice sounded so familiar." She wasn't aware of what she was saying; she was tired and nervous, and she must have been hearing things. Voice sound different in the dark, she told herself. Don't be a fool.

"Yeah . . . well, like I said . . . I thought I knew you,

too. I guess people are always thinking they knew somebody before."

She was caught in the grip of a confusion she didn't understand. I should go home, she thought. I'm too tired to make any sense.

"Yes. Of course," was all she could manage.

"Look," Tom began awkwardly, "I was supposed to meet a bunch of people . . . I mean we're having a big party, but I'm kinda late . . ."

"Oh, I'm sorry," said Betty immediately. "Thank you so much for helping me, and forgive me for detaining you."

"No, what I mean is . . . I mean . . . all of a sudden I don't feel like going to a big party. So I mean . . . if you're not in any hurry, uh . . . would you like to have a cup of coffee . . . or something? . . ." He waited anxiously for her answer, but she didn't say a word. She stood there staring at him.

"I guess not, huh?"

Betty Logan stared at the tall young man with the disappointed face. As clearly as if they were being spoken now, she could hear the words that had been eluding her. ". . . if someday somebody came up to you . . . and he acted like he'd seen you before . . . he might even be a football player . . . you'd notice that same thing. I mean . . . even if you only thought you did, you'd give him a chance, wouldn't you? He might be a good guy . . ."

"You're the quarterback, aren't you?" she asked suddenly.

"Yeah!" Tom smiled, pleased. "Now, how did you know that?"

Betty shook her head helplessly. "I don't know," she admitted, spreading her hands out. "There's something about you I recognized." She hesitated, then said slowly, "Yes. I'd love to have a cup of coffee with you."

He grinned at her, and they walked out onto the

field, where the last of the stadium lights were slowly being turned off.

Neither one of them saw the dark-eyed man who watched them go, his smile gentle and approving. But how could they? Even Max Corkle had never actually laid eyes on Mr. Jordan.